SHATTERED

NIGHTWIND PACK BOOK 2

LAURANN DOHNER

KELE MOON

Editor: Kelli Collins

Cover Artist: Dar Albert

ISBN: 978-1-7342109-1-0

PROLOGUE

THE PAST

*I*t was the sound that drew Amber Daniels from her hideout beneath the massive roots of a tree near her house. Not the loud screech of brakes, but rather, the horrible thump after it.

In seconds, tires squealed again, and the engine roared louder before the car sped away. Amber set her doll down carefully on her sweater to avoid Molly getting dirty and climbed out of her secret spot. She darted fearful glances around to make sure her stepdad wasn't within sight and crept toward the backwoods road.

It was empty as usual, but a soft whining noise had her turning away from the street and searching through the thick brush next to it. She instantly spotted the puppy lying there, panting heavily. His black fur appeared wet and she knew, even at six years old, what had happened. He'd been struck by a car, and she could tell he was very injured. The person had just taken off and left him to die.

"Oh no," she whispered.

She wasn't sure why she knew it was a puppy when this black dog was easily as big as a hunting hound. He had huge paws, as if he hadn't grown into them yet and a cute, pet-able look of a pup that made her want to reach out and touch him.

He whined again and lifted his head. Big, bright blue eyes locked on her. She moved forward and dropped to her knees next to him, knowing it was a bad idea to approach a wild dog.

Amber decided puppies were okay.

"I'm with you," she crooned softly, knowing he would probably die from how badly he bled. She reached out and gently touched his hind leg that didn't appear hurt. She brushed her fingertips through his soft black fur, hoping to soothe him. "Don't be afraid. I'd never hurt you."

Tears welled up in her eyes, blinding her when the puppy dropped his head and let out another pained whine. She inched closer to stroke his head but was sure to be careful of his big jaws. She knew now why this puppy was so huge. He wasn't a dog, but a wolf. She'd seen the wild wolves come out of the woods a few times. Usually her stepdad fired off one of his shotguns to scare them away, muttering about how dangerous they were, but this one didn't seem mean. Her gaze lingered on his side when she saw how labored his breathing had become.

"I could get my mommy." She petted the top of his head. "Maybe she could help. I don't want you to die. She's a grown-up and probably knows what to do to save you."

It happened fast. The thick black fur on his head turned into something thinner and silkier. The pup's body changed. His fur receded.

In a few blinks, a boy lay curled on his side, naked and covered in blood by his hip and rib area.

"Don't," he whispered. "Please? I'll heal."

Amber's mouth opened but nothing came out. The boy appeared to be about nine years old. He turned his head to look at her and his eyes were the same stunning blue as a human as they'd been in wolf form. Her fingers were entangled in his shoulder-length hair. She'd never seen a boy with such long hair, but then, she'd never seen a wolf turn into a boy, either.

"Please don't tell anyone," he rasped while Amber tried to find her voice. "They'll either kill me or lock me up inside a cage to study me."

She knew he told her the truth, that he was different, and she didn't want anyone to hurt him. "You need help," she finally whispered.

"I'm different from you. I'll heal. I just need time."

"Are you sure?" She doubted it when her gaze darted to the blood on his side.

"I'm sure." He sounded confident despite the quiver of pain in his voice. "Please don't tell anyone."

She glanced back to his face, mesmerized by those intense eyes. "I swear I won't. What can I do? I have water."

"Ams?" The male voice came from the woods behind her.

Fear spread through her, and she could tell from the look on the injured boy's face that he was scared, too. Amber bit her lip. "That's my stepdad. He can't find you. If I help you, do you think you can walk just right over there?" She pointed to her tree. "I have a hiding place. He won't find us there. He hasn't found me yet."

The boy let her assist him to his feet, leaning on her heavily, being sure to keep his injured side away from her. He was really heavy and so much taller than her. He limped, and it slowed them down, but they reached the dying tree.

"Right there." She gestured to her hiding spot. "There's a big hole hidden between the roots and I've been digging out the space under it since I was little. The bushes in front keep it hidden. There's water and some of my things inside. He won't find us."

"Ams? Where the hell are you?" Her stepdad sounded closer, louder and angrier. "I don't got all day to look for your dumb ass."

Amber stepped around the bushes, exposing the hole between the roots, and helped him crawl inside. Once she sat down, she turned to face the boy who was curled on his side again. She avoided looking at his body as much as she could, since she didn't want to embarrass him. She would be so scared if she found herself naked in front of a stranger. She used a blanket to cover him from thigh to hip, hiding his backside. Then grabbed her sweater from the corner and rolled it up to put under his head.

"Ams, you little pain in the ass! Where the hell are you?"

The wolf-boy looked at her, eyes almost too bright in the semi-darkness, but now he seemed more curious than scared. "Your name is Ams?"

"Amber," she said automatically, like she was in school. "What's your name?"

"Desmon, but, um—" He swallowed hard. "My friends call me Des."

She poured some water into one of the tea cups she played with and held it up to his lips. He drank and then lay his head down. She hesitated before running her fingers through his long, silky hair again. Sometimes, when she was sick, her mom did that for her and it made her feel a little better.

"Goddamn it, I'm going to blister your ass if you don't come out!" Her stepdad's voice came from farther away. "Don't test me, brat! It'll make the belt you got last week look like a tap!"

Desmon glanced worriedly toward the covered opening to her hideout. "You should go before he calls the police and they hunt for you."

She shook her head. "He won't do that. He grows plants I'm not supposed to tell anyone about, and the police would find them. I hide a lot, but I'll go home when he's sober."

The boy frowned. "Sober?"

"He drinks." She looked away from him, feeling embarrassed. "I broke something and he's mad. I'll stay here tonight, and he'll forget in the morning. He usually does."

They stared at each other, before Desmon warned her, "If you ever tell anyone what you saw, they *will* hunt me."

She stopped combing her fingers through his hair. "I give you my ultimate pinkie promise that I'll never tell anyone in my whole life about you, Des. I don't want anyone to hurt you. You're nice."

"I just need to rest. I'll get better. Stay with me." Desmon relaxed and closed his eyes. "Talk to me."

She stroked his hair again. "What grade are you in?"

"Grade?" His tone was heavier, like he was already falling asleep.

"For school? How old are you?"

"Six." He pulled the blanket up tighter around him. "No school, but we have classes. Hunting classes. Tracking classes."

Amber had thought he was much older, like nine, but knowing he was her age was nice because she didn't have any friends in her grade. Even if he was the biggest six-year-old she'd ever met, she still liked him. Too bad he couldn't go to school with her since he seemed to live nearby.

"You don't do math?" Amber was sort of jealous. "Or reading?"

"My mom teaches us math. She makes us read too." Desmon didn't sound too excited about it. "Pups in Goodwin don't have to read, but Nightwinds do—all the time, every day. They make fun of us."

"Kids make fun of me too," she admitted softly, but she wasn't sure if he heard her because his hand dropped to his side.

Amber felt his chest. He was still breathing.

Desmon slept.

It grew darker, colder, and Amber curled up against him to keep warm. She feared he had a fever when she realized how hot his skin felt compared to hers.

She didn't have any friends. Maybe he could stay with her and she could sneak him food, and he could start going to real school with her to stay away from the mean kids who teased him.

She drifted to sleep—and discovered him gone in the morning when she woke up.

She was alone...again.

Two days later, completely healed, a huge black wolf pup with blue eyes showed up to play with her.

She never told anyone about Desmon.

Almost Ten Years Later

"Amber?"

She cringed, huddling in the small space hidden between the massive tree roots. They had worked to expand their hideout over the years by digging it out more, but it was still a little too small. Her long blonde hair fell over her face when she dropped her head.

In seconds, the bushes rustled and Desmon climbed into the tight space. He bumped her shoulder in a playful, wolf-like gesture.

She winced but bit her lip rather than let him know how sore she was. "Hi." She refused to look at him.

"Sorry I'm late." He held out a handful of wildflowers. "Are you mad?"

"No. They're beautiful." She took the bouquet with her good hand and smelled them. She liked the little nature gifts Desmon always brought her. "Thank you."

"I can't stay long." He sighed. "It's my birthday."

"I know." She set the flowers down, reached into her lap and lifted the present she had wrapped for him. "Did you really think I'd forget you turning sixteen?"

"A gift?" He sounded stunned. "You didn't have to do this."

She peeked at him in the dim light glimmering between the strands of hair she was hiding behind. "I know you said you were going to be real busy today but I'm glad you made it."

He reached out and squeezed her hand. "I always keep my promises to you."

"I know you do." Amber stared at her small hand in his larger one and her heart ached. She wasn't sure when it had happened, but Desmon had become everything to her. He was the one shining light in her bleak life, but she didn't get to see him much. He said his people, the ones like him, wouldn't allow him to be around full humans. He rarely got the chance to sneak away to see her, now that he was older and they had given him more duties after his father died. "I wanted to bake you a cake, but—"

"It's all right." He tore open the packaging—and then paused, staring at her gift. "Ams, I can't accept this. It's too much."

A human boy might think the gift was stupid, but Desmon was different. She got the impression that, like her family, his people didn't have much. Or more likely, didn't *need* much. He was never interested in the latest video games or cool cars like the boys she went to school with.

She bit her lip again. "You can't refuse a gift I made just for you."

"You're so talented." He caressed the delicate carving of a wolf that looked amazingly similar to Desmon in his changed form. "This must have taken you weeks to do."

Months, but she didn't correct him. It was the best piece she'd ever created, and it had cost her more than time. Her stepdad had found it and wanted to sell it for booze to one of the shops in town. When she'd snatched it back from him, he'd started beating on her, trying to pry it from her fingers because she refused to let it go.

She had bruises, but she'd gotten away with Desmon's wolf.

"It's from a piece of the root of this tree, to make it extra special."

Desmon reached for her hand, took it and lifted her fingers to his lips. He brushed a kiss there. "Thank you."

"I wanted you to have something to remind you of me when we're apart."

"You're always with me in my thoughts." His voice turned a little gruff, inhumanly so, and she'd noticed it had started happening more often in the past few months. He closed his eyes and admitted, "I think about you all the time."

She smiled, her heart warming. "I wish you were allowed to go into town, so I could accidentally run into you sometimes."

"We're not permitted to mingle with humans. We allow a few to live near our land to keep us hidden from bigger developers, but we aren't supposed to talk to them."

"I know." She tried not to complain. She'd never tell him how bleak her life really was, but she couldn't help but confess, "I just miss you."

"When you hit maturity..." He paused, as if he'd said something he shouldn't.

Amber's heart rate sped up. She knew that word translated into adulthood in Desmon speak. "Yes?"

He tightened his big hand over hers.

"I want you, Amber," he said with a growl, his voice dropping to a deep and husky tone that sent a shiver over her body. "I can't stop thinking about it."

She turned to him, forgetting why she'd been hiding her cheek. "How?"

Desmon dropped her hand and suddenly had her face cradled in his calloused palms. She stared into his startling eyes, surprised to see fury reflected in the sapphire orbs. Even the shape of them physically changed, making him seem more animalistic despite being in human form.

"Who did this to you?"

She blinked back hot tears, because the bruises weren't new. The rest, however

"How do you want me, Des? Are you talking about sex?"

He studied her, his eyes still making him look primal, his voice completely inhuman as he demanded, "Who hit you, Amber? Your stepfather? I'll tear him apart for touching my mate!"

His mate.

Those words shot straight to her heart. "Are you asking me to marry you?"

Desmon's chest rose and fell with harsh, panting breaths as he asked again, "Is he the one who struck you?"

She reached up, wincing as she moved her shoulder and gripped his hands with hers. "I'm fine. I tripped," she lied. "I didn't want to ruin your birthday by letting you see me this way."

"Don't protect him." His eyes changed even more as he spoke, and his canine teeth grew longer in his mouth. "He doesn't deserve it."

"You're losing your human face."

"He's lucky I have a human face at all." His voice was still a growl of fury. "I should be ripping his throat out right now. If he were one of my people, he'd already be dead. I don't like males who abuse women, especially *my woman*. No one is allowed to hurt you, Amber, you're the one nice part of my life. I'd kill for you in a heartbeat."

She wasn't afraid of the confession.

Amber knew Desmon wouldn't hurt her. More so, despite evidence to the contrary, she knew he was good, though others might think she was crazy for that. He threatened violence a lot, especially when he got angry and lost control of his features, but he wouldn't actually kill.

Even if he was part animal.

He never said the word, but she knew he was a werewolf. Those mystical creatures that weren't supposed to exist. But Desmon was startlingly real to her. He was the only thing she could trust as decent and good, so she didn't question him. She knew he wasn't allowed to tell humans anything, and she respected him enough to let it go.

She caressed his face, hoping to calm him down. "Are you asking me to marry you when we hit eighteen?"

He nodded, even though his breathing was still labored. "Yes."

"Yes?" She smiled hopefully.

Desmon reached out to her, caressing her cheek once more. "I wish I could take you away with me now, but I can't until you turn eighteen. They'd search for you, and my people won't allow me to hide you until you're fully mature by your world's standards."

"I love you, Des," she confessed as tears rolled down her cheeks from the onslaught of emotions. "But I wasn't sure you felt the same way about me. You've never even tried to kiss me."

"I've wanted to, but my people aren't good at curbing our instincts." He slid his hand from her cheek to her throat, and then traced his finger down the curve of it. Desmon caressed her pulse point as his gaze dropped lower, to the V-cut of her shirt. His pupils were still dilated and wild looking, but she knew he was feeling primal for a different reason, his voice still more of a growl. "I just can't risk it until you're ready to mate. Everything in me wants you—all sides. You have been the biggest test of my control. You've made me stronger than I ever thought I could be."

She laughed. "Really?"

"You have no idea, Angel." Desmon groaned and released her to look away as if he were trying to gather his strength. "I ache for you until it hurts. In a year and a half, on your birthday, I'm going to come for you and take you to our home."

A warm, hopeful excitement spread over her in a way that was both foreign and wholly addictive. "That's amazing. I wish I could see where you live."

"No, it's too dangerous right now to take you into pack territory, and I won't risk your life." He looked genuinely regretful to disappoint her. "I told you that my people would hurt you if they knew about our relationship, just the way your people would hurt *me*. When we finally mate, my people will accept you. It's a natural law, once you're mature in your world, and our leaders, even the corrupt ones, are forced to obey any law governed by nature. We just have to wait a little longer. My mother was like you before she met my father, and my people loved her. I promise, once you're eighteen, we can be together every day."

"I don't even know what you are," she said hesitantly, because she hadn't known his mother was human—or used to be.

He quirked a dark eyebrow at her. "Does it matter? Will a label change how you feel about me? About us?"

"No." Amber shook her head. "I love you. Whatever you are, I still love you."

He nodded, before he winced in disappointment. "I have to go."

"So soon?" She hated when he left, saying goodbye was torture. "You just got here."

"I know, but they're having a special ceremony for my birthday." He didn't look very excited about it. "I have to be there before the sun goes down."

"What kind of ceremony?"

"I don't know. It's been kept a secret." He avoided looking at her, as though he was suddenly uncomfortable. "I'm a little different from most of my people."

"How?" Amber gave him her best pleading look and batted her

eyelashes, knowing how he would react. "Can you at least answer that?"

"All right." He laughed, making Amber feel trusted when he told her, "My father was an alpha, and I'm his only pup. He wants my loyalty to keep the peace, and I have a lot of good reasons to resist giving it to him. So, it's probably something to do with that."

She stared at Desmon's wide shoulders. He stood at just over six-foot-three and was easily over two hundred pounds of muscled, wide-shouldered male. She thought he'd been a few grades higher than her when they'd first met, but he had just been a *really* big kid.

It was difficult to take in that he wasn't done growing yet, since that was obviously what he meant about the maturity thing. "Can you sneak away before the end of the month this time?"

"I'll try." He paused, still looking miserable. "The alpha has had his men keeping watch on me. I had to lose five other wolves in the woods to get to you. Wherever I go, they attempt to follow."

Amber hesitated, and then leaned forward. She stole a kiss, but it was innocent, just her lips brushing against his warm cheek. "Happy birthday, Des."

He closed his eyes, inhaling in her scent, and softly growled. "Too close."

"You always say that." She pulled back, even if everything in her protested it. "When we were kids, you used to let me climb all over you, and you used to let me to curl up with you, too."

"When we were kids, I didn't have the strong urges I do now." His blue eyes noticeably darkened. "You wouldn't want to cuddle with me if you knew what I wanted to do to you."

"I know about sex, Des."

He growled again, and anger suddenly tightened his features. "Did a male touch you?"

"No. The only one I want is you, but we have television." She shrugged, feeling her cheeks heat from the low growl of possessiveness in his voice before she added, "And I read books."

"I've never touched a female because I only want you." His body relaxed, as if the thought alone was enough to calm his wild side. "Will you promise me the same? Will you save yourself for me?"

Amber gave him a smile. "Yes."

Desmon breathed a deep, heavy sigh of a relief and smiled back at her.

"I love my gift." He cradled the wood carving in his palm. "I have to go. The sun is setting, and I have miles to run."

She nodded. "Go."

He left as quickly as he'd arrived. She waited about five minutes and then walked to the tree across the old road. Desmon's discarded clothing waited there, as always, but the carving wasn't on the ground. She grinned and hoped his wolf teeth didn't damage the wood when he ran home.

She bent, folded the pants and shirt, and then returned his clothes to the bag she used to protect them from the forest. She moved the rock, hid the bag inside the hole she'd dug, and pushed the rock back into place. The next time he came, they would be waiting for him.

She grinned with the knowledge that Desmon wanted to marry her. As soon as she hit eighteen, she was going to start a new life with him.

That was all she ever wanted.

She turned—and her heart nearly stopped in terror when she found herself staring at three naked men standing silently in the woods within ten feet of her.

They didn't look similar to Desmon with their fairer skin tones and lighter hair, but she *knew* what they were.

They were like Desmon.

She swallowed hard. The one closest to her sniffed, grimaced, and narrowed green eyes at her. "Human."

"Is he toying with her?" the one to his left grunted.

"She doesn't smell of him."

"Albert will want to see her. He'll want to know who she is and what Desmon was doing with her."

She was in trouble, and Amber knew it. She didn't need animal instincts to sense the danger. Her heart pounded as she took off, sprinting for the road.

One of them grabbed her painfully around her waist before she could get far, hauling her up off her feet with a furious snarl.

The sound terrified her more.

"Where do you think you're going, rabbit?" His sharp teeth threatened her skin as he dragged his mouth over her throat, drool dripping on her from his parted lips. "Mmmm. Too bad we can't just kill her now. After Albert is done, I say we play with her. I love the taste of their blood. It's fun watching them die."

Amber opened her mouth and screamed.

1

THE PRESENT — FOURTEEN YEARS LATER

*A*mber jerked into a sitting position in the bed, panting. It took a while for her to realize she was safe. Even after she did, she kept taking deep breaths, trying to slow her heart rate while cursing to herself.

She hadn't relived that day in years.

The bedroom door jerked open, spilling light into the room when her younger half-sister Beatrice rushed in. "Are you all right?"

"Shit. I screamed, didn't I?"

She nodded. "What is it? Did you see a spider? I hate those things."

"No. Sorry." Amber shoved the covers off. "I had a nightmare."

Bea gave her a strained smile. "It must've been epic."

"Yeah. It was pretty bad." Amber turned on the bedside lamp and took note of the time. "How's Mom?"

"The nurse still has her pretty drugged." Bea lowered her head, looking more overwhelmed and sadder than a seventeen-year-old girl ever should. "I was actually about to wake you up. I don't think she's going to make it through the night."

Pain lanced through Amber. She'd arrived the day before to the childhood home she swore she'd never return to, after getting the call letting her know that her mother had been sent home from the hospital to die in her own bed.

Amber just nodded. "Okay. The three of us will sit with her then until the end comes."

"Katie isn't here." Bea paused. "She's not answering her phone, either. I know where she is, and I called like a thousand times, but they won't put her on. Just told me to text her."

"What do you mean they won't put her on the phone?"

A blush rose up on Bea's cheeks. "She's at The Barn. Her boyfriend hangs out there, and he enjoys it when she's with him. He probably told the bartender to hang up on me, so she won't leave."

"The Barn? Isn't that the bar at the base of Hollow Mountain?"

"That's where she hangs out."

"She's not twenty-one yet."

Bea shrugged. "They don't care."

"What do you mean by that? Aren't they worried about their liquor license?"

"No." Bea snorted like the idea was ridiculous. "If Roni were at work, she would kick Katie out like she usually does, but it's her night off. I have her personal number, and I texted her, but she didn't answer. She's probably out on a date or something."

"I'll call the bar."

"The bartender got sick of me and took the phone off the hook. I even had the operator try, and she confirmed it." Tears filled Bea's eyes. "Katie won't be here when Mom dies, and she'll never forgive herself."

"I'll go get her."

Bea hesitated. "Um..."

"What?" Amber walked over to her open suitcase placed on the chair and grabbed a pair of jeans.

"It's kind of a rough place. There are a lot of bikers there."

"Then Katie definitely has no business being there at eleven o'clock at night, or at any time, for that matter. Mom allowed that?"

"Yeah, but you know how bad Mom's drinking has been."

"Not really."

"After Daddy moved out and took up with that new woman, well, drinking is all she does. She didn't really care what we did as long as she had booze."

Rage boiled under Amber's skin, making her face feel flush. She tore off her nightgown and dressed quickly. "I'll go get Katie. I remember how to get to the bar. Your dad used to get shitfaced there sometimes and we'd have to go get him."

"Ams, it's rough." Bea sounded far too worldly wise for a teenager. "I mean, some of the men who hang there are criminals—for real."

"I spent eight years married to Jeff." She smirked. "Trust me. I know all about those types."

"He introduced you to his clients?"

She shrugged as she slipped on a pair of heels to give her height and hopefully make herself a little more intimidating. "Socializing with clients is part of a defense attorney's life. Sometimes we had parties, and I had to meet a few of the men he represented. It was my duty to entertain them."

"I really hated Jeff. He treated you as though you were his slave instead of his wife."

Amber grabbed her purse and met her younger sister's eyes. "We all make mistakes. I thought he was someone he could never be, and he thought I'd put up with anything he did."

"I'm still glad you screwed him in the divorce settlement."

"The judge presiding over our case didn't feel too generous toward him when it came out that he had four girlfriends he supported in those so-called rental properties."

"You never suspected?"

"He worked all the time. I believed him, until I found out he'd gotten a woman pregnant."

"Was the baby his?"

Pain still burned in her chest over the betrayal. "He's paying child support, so I assume it is. He refused to allow me to have a baby. He kept putting me off when I begged him to start a family, but then he goes and knocks up one of his legal secretaries? I guess he put in more than overtime at the office."

"I'm sorry," Bea said earnestly. "And I really don't think it's a good idea for you to go to The Barn."

Amber shrugged. "I'm past the pain and anger stage with Jeff. Now I'm in the 'so over it' stage. Good timing. I can handle some small-town punks. I've lived in Los Angeles for fourteen years."

"Okay." Bea looked less than certain. "Please be careful, Amber. Remember that if they look mean, and they act mean, they *are* mean —so stay away."

Fifteen minutes later, Amber pulled into the parking lot of The Barn. She glanced at the motorcycles, tricked-out trucks and muscle cars around her. She sighed loudly and unfastened her seat belt. Then she leaned across the center console and opened her glove box. She wrapped her fingers around the mace, straightened, took a deep breath, and then climbed out of her car.

Twenty-year-old Katie was in that bar, and fury went a long way toward Amber finding the courage to march into the large old building.

Music loudly thumped as she stepped inside and let her gaze sweep the room. To the left sat a bar being tended by a long-haired man in a tank top with tattoos showing down both arms. He looked up and their gazes locked. She frowned at him, and then her attention moved on.

Tables were filled with mostly men. The dress code seemed to be jeans, t-shirts and leather jackets. *Great*, she thought. *A wannabe biker bar in the middle-of-nowhere, Northern California.*

One of the women dancing in front of a table drew her attention, but she was older, a brunette, and definitely not Amber's baby half-sister. The skirt the woman wore rose so high, the lower line of her ass showed as she wiggled and bent while moving to the rock tune.

Two more women were in the back near the pool tables. A third woman was pinned behind a big man in a black metal band t-shirt. Amber couldn't see much of her since she happened to be heavily making out with her partner. The huge man dropped his arm and reached down to grab the woman's jean-skirt-clad ass.

Amber saw the short blonde hair—and anger surged through her as she stormed over to her sister.

A guy at a table stood from his chair and stepped in her path. She froze, stared up at him, and suddenly felt tiny at five-foot-four in her two-inch heels. He was a big son of a bitch, a beefy man with a lot of facial hair.

He smiled. "Hey, baby."

Amber nearly stumbled back from his whiskey-soaked breath.

"Excuse me." She tried to step around him, but he moved in her path. "I'm here for someone."

He grabbed her arm. "I'm someone."

"*Someone else*," she clarified with an unimpressed look.

"Now don't be a bitch." His smile broadened, showing off straight white teeth that were surprising, considering how rough around the edges the rest of him looked. "Or be a bitch. I do like them."

Men nearby laughed, and Amber had to force herself to push down the fear. She lifted her chin, leveled her coldest glare at him and jerked her arm free.

"First off, I hate that term. It's rude. Second, if you touch me again, you're going to regret it. Now, please move out of the way while I collect my sister."

He cocked his head, staring at her, and then glanced over his shoulder. He faced her again. "Who's your sister?"

"Katie."

His eyes widened, and he slowly gave her a once-over, from the high heels she wore to her face. "You got the looks." He grinned. "She's taken, but you're not."

The biker poster child reached for her again.

Amber raised her arm, showing off the small canister in her hand, and gave him a pointed look. "See this? It's mace. Back off and get out of my way."

He frowned but took a step back. He leaned forward and sniffed the mace curiously, which was odd, but nothing about him seemed normal in the first place. Amber moved, heading quickly for the couple still making out in the corner. She was shocked as she watched the guy lift her sister and pin her to the wall, before he slid his hand between their bodies.

"Katie!"

Her sister jerked in the man's arms and turned toward Amber. Astonishment transformed Katie's features instantly and her mouth hung open in shock. "Ams? What in the hell are you doing here?"

Drawing to a halt, Amber fought the urge to yell at her sister for making out with a guy in a bar in front of an audience. She tried hard to remember that her sister was over eighteen, a perfectly legal adult, but her temper won.

"You need to come home with me now. Mom has taken a turn for the worse."

Amber regretted just spitting that out when she saw her younger sister's face pale.

"Let me down, Merl." Katie pushed on his chest. "I've got to go."

"No. You can leave when I'm done. I'm rock hard and I'm going to fuck you."

Did he really just say that to my sister? Yes, he did. Amber's mind worked but her mouth didn't. She was stunned speechless.

Katie wiggled against the wall and pushed on his chest. "Not in front of my sister. Come on, stud. I'll come back. You heard her. It's my mom."

The big jerk shook his head. "Now. Fuck first, then you can go."

Katie bit her lip and turned her head, staring at her sister. "Go home to sit with Mom, and I'll be there real soon."

"Are you joking?" Amber's eyes widened. "Come with me *right now.*"

"I can't. I promised Merl some of my time. I've been ignoring him."

Amber's heart nearly stopped. "Is he..." Horror and dread washed through her. "Is he paying you?"

"No." Katie genuinely looked offended. "I'm not a hooker. How could you think that?"

The man holding her sister chuckled. "She's mine, and unlike the rest of your kind, she doesn't care where I fuck her."

Amber turned her head, gawking at the grinning men around them who watched the scene unfold as if it were amusing. She looked back to her sister and saw how much paler Katie's face had become. She also saw guilt in her sister's eyes.

"Katie?" She paused, getting a grip on her conflicting emotions. "You're an adult, and I'm trying very hard to not freak out, but I am not leaving here without you." She glared at the man pinning her sister. "Please put my sister down, or I'll force you to."

He laughed, glancing at Katie. "I like her. She's funny." His grin died as he shot Amber a glare. "I'm going to nail your little sis to the wall right here and right now. You look a little prudish, so maybe you can learn something when you watch me do it. Then maybe I'll give you a chance to show everyone what you learned."

The jerk went for Katie's mouth and tried to kiss her. Her sister shoved at him, turning her head to avoid his seeking lips, and Amber moved without giving it any thought. That man refused to let her sister go, so she grabbed the pool stick from a table.

She distantly heard someone call out, but she hit the guy before his friends could warn him. It broke across his broad back. He cursed loudly, dropped her sister and spun to face his attacker —Amber.

She sprayed him in the face with mace.

He roared out so loudly that it hurt Amber's ears. She'd never heard someone make that sound. She dropped the mace in shock as the big man frantically clawed at his face and spun away, crashing into one of the four pool tables. He hit it, bent over and roared out in pain again.

"Oh my God! Run!" Katie shouted and grabbed her arm. "You don't know what you just did!"

Amber stumbled as her sister jerked on her, but her legs were suddenly frozen when a snarl tore from the man and he pushed up to confront her. Amber couldn't look away from his face. Tears streamed down his cheeks. Hair sprouted from his cheeks, chin and arms. His mouth opened and he roared; an animalistic, terrifying sound as his watery, enraged gaze fixed on her.

He flashed deadly canine teeth that had grown long in a way she'd seen before. Then he came at her—fast.

Amber couldn't move to protect herself. He wasn't human, but she could wager a good guess what he was. He started to change before her eyes, confirming it for her, as someone leapt in his path.

Katie threw out her arms to protect her. "Please don't, Merl! She didn't know."

Merl backhanded Katie in the shoulder, shoving her away rather than attack, but then he reached for Amber, making it obvious she wouldn't be so lucky.

One second Amber stood there in horror, and the next she'd landed flat on her back. The pain shocked her. It had been a long time since she'd been beaten. She wasn't sure if she was struggling to breathe through the memories of her childhood, or because Merl knocked all the air out of her. Then a weight crushed down on her chest when he landed on top of her, making it even more impossible to catch her breath.

She fought to get air into her lungs and her eyes opened wide to stare up in pure terror at the thing on top of her. His arm rose, and her gaze flew to it on instinct. Sharp claws were out, a few inches longer than his fingertips, and then he swiped at her.

Katie threw herself onto his back, grabbing his arm. He missed Amber's cheek by inches as his hand slammed against the floor next to her.

"Please!" Katie screamed. "She's my sister!"

Katie straddled the guy's back, draping herself over him. Amber's gaze locked with her sister's. She saw how terrified Katie was; moreover, she knew she probably had that exact same expression.

"Please, baby," Katie sobbed. "For me? Don't hurt her. She didn't know. She thought she was protecting me."

He snarled, glaring at Amber. "I won't kill her."

"Thank you." Katie released his arm and wrapped her own around his chest, hugging him. "Thank you, Merl. I owe you, and I'll make it up to you somehow."

He didn't look away from Amber once as he studied her with

those watery, primal-looking eyes, making her feel like prey. "No. *She* owes me, and she's going to pay for what she did."

"No, no, no," Katie begged. "Not that, baby. She's too old and you don't want her."

He softly snarled. "I won't kill her, but I could change my mind. Off me *now*. Don't interfere."

"I'll do anything, Merl." Katie rubbed his chest. "She wouldn't be any fun. She would just scream and cry. I'll love anything you want to do to me."

He shook his head. "*Her*."

"No!"

He turned his head, breaking eye contact with Amber and put his sharp teeth a breath away from Katie's face as he roared, "Get off now!"

Katie released him, slid off his back and stood. Tears streamed down her face. "Please, Merl? I'll beg! I'll get on my knees right here."

Wolf howls filled the room, and Amber's heart nearly stopped as she turned her head enough to see the room from her position on the floor. At least thirty men and the handful of women had surrounding them. All of them were standing there watching and making those loud noises.

If pure fear could have killed her, she knew in that second she'd be dead. *It isn't just Merl who's a werewolf.*

Like a scene out of a horror movie, the entire bar seemed to be full of them.

"Her," Merl demanded in a low, inhuman voice.

A sob filled the room as Katie backed away. "Please don't kill her."

Amber glanced back at her sister, who kept slowly retreating. Their gazes locked.

"Don't fight. He'll hurt you." Katie sniffed, hugging her chest. "I'm so sorry. I can't do anything."

Katie spun around, faced the wall and didn't move.

Amber looked to the creature crouched on all fours, pinning her to the floor with his heavy body. His eyes were still more animal than human when he snarled at her, showing off his deadly teeth. Merl lifted his hand as he lowered his focus to her chest.

A whimper came from Amber when his claws lightly raked the front of her shirt between her breasts. She glanced down right as the material separated, and he used the sharp points to cut open her shirt.

"You wanted to play with me? Now it's *my* turn to play with you." He bent forward, his teeth coming closer to her face, and drool dripped from his open mouth to splatter on the skin between her breasts that he'd bared. "You attacked me so I wouldn't fuck your sister. The good news is, I don't want her right now." He paused, a claw sliding between her ribs and the front bra clasp that held the cups together. He gave it a tug and sliced it open. "The bad news is, I'm going to fuck *you*—and you are going to enjoy it as much as I did that mace."

Howls echoed off the walls again.

A sudden loud crash sounded throughout the room, and Merl jerked his head up. His pupils dilated more, but it looked different somehow, like a dog who was suddenly scared.

"What the hell is going on?" a man snarled in a deep, truly scary voice.

Katie spun around and dropped to her knees. "I beg you, Alpha! My sister was only trying to protect me. I don't have my phone, or I would've called you. Please don't let Merl hurt her!"

"Bea is here? Merl? What the hell?" A roar tore through the room that was twice as intimidating as Merl's fury. "Get off that little girl!" Another snarl sounded as the voice grew closer. "Why did you bring her here, Katie? Only you're allowed, damn it, and I don't even think *you* should be here!"

"It's not Bea," Merl grunted but didn't budge. "She's still seventeen, and I don't touch them underage."

"Katie only has the one sister." The voice grew deeper, angrier.

"I have an older one." Katie sniffed. "She just got to town yesterday because of my mom being sick. I forgot my phone in Merl's truck, and she must've driven down here when she couldn't get ahold of me. Please, Alpha, I'm pleading with you. She attacked Merl thinking she was saving me."

"I didn't know you had an older sister." The voice became less deep, easier to understand as some of the anger left his tone. "Release her *now*."

Merl softly growled as he stared at Amber petulantly. "I have your scent, bitch. I'll be seeing you soon. You owe me some pain."

"I said release her!"

Movement drew Amber's attention, and she caught a glimpse of the other man's boots when he walked up behind Merl. A second later, Merl ended up torn away from her. His large body sailed a good six feet before he crashed onto the floor hard.

Amber lay there motionless, staring at the back of the man who had just saved her. He had long black hair that fell past his broad shoulders. His arms were muscular, thick and bulky as they stretched the material of his blue t-shirt. His bare feet showed under his jeans, as if he'd stormed out of the house without shoes, and his hands remained fisted at his sides. He growled at Merl when the man sat up.

"You don't hurt women, especially not...*fragile ones* like this!"

Amber got the impression he'd stopped short of saying "human ones."

"I'm sorry, Alpha." Merl lowered his head, staring at the floor submissively. "I'm just pissed."

Some of the other men in the bar laughed, and one mimicked in a high girly voice, "*I'm sorry, Alpha.*"

Another man said, "Nightwind are *all* bitches, not just the women."

The long-haired man growled. His voice was low and dangerous when he asked, "What was that? I'd love a dominance fight with a Goodwin right now. Give me a reason, Buck. Please."

"Nothing." The two men mocking them looked away, as though they were afraid to make eye contact.

"She sprayed me with mace," Merl explained when the attention focused back on him. "It was instinct to protect myself from the human, Alpha."

The long-haired man snorted. "I'm sure you deserved it."

The alpha turned then, facing Amber—and she got a look at a pair of hauntingly beautiful blue eyes set against the backdrop of the same handsome face she'd dreamed about for most of her life.

She was grateful she was still lying on the floor because her entire body went lax from shock, though she wasn't sure why.

She should've expected him the second bikers started sprouting fur.

His eyes widened with the same recognition, and he stumbled back a step, his gaze never leaving hers.

Amber jerked, startled, when he suddenly leapt at her without warning in a way a human would never be able to do. He landed on all fours on top of her, not touching, but very close. His body was inches above hers, and he lowered his face until they were nearly nose to nose. Desmon stared into her eyes, and she couldn't look away from him. The blue was much brighter than she remembered, and she swallowed hard against the lump that formed in her throat when the emotion overwhelmed her.

"Hi, Des." Her voice was barely a whisper.

He closed his eyes and turned his head, inhaling slowly, as if savoring whatever he was smelling.

Then a deep, angry growl tore from his throat as his eyes opened. He didn't look at her face but instead at her sliced-open shirt and the exposed bra cups that barely contained her breasts since the clasp had been cut. His gaze rose to lock with hers.

"Don't move," he snarled.

In the blink of an eye, he was off her, on his feet, and he had Merl by his throat. The other man screamed as he was thrown. He hit the wall hard enough to break the plaster where he impacted a good ten feet away.

Desmon snarled and then turned back, pure rage in his gaze as he stared down at Amber again. He turned his head, glaring at Merl.

"If you'd hurt her, I would've killed you. Slowly. *She's off limits*." He looked around the room, his piercing-blue stare pausing on each of the people standing there, now shuffling uncomfortably. "Is that understood? One drop of her blood or the scent of her terror and you will die. She's under my protection."

"Thank you, Alpha." Katie got to her feet. "We owe you a debt."

"Go home to your mother," Desmon ordered like he expected her to obey.

Katie nodded and walked toward Amber. "We're leaving. Thank you."

"Don't," Desmon demanded softly. "You go. She stays. She's safe."

Katie opened her mouth, looking genuinely shocked, but Desmon growled low at her. Katie nodded and backed away, shooting a fearful glance in Amber's direction.

In seconds, her sister fled the bar, and Amber's full focus fixed on Desmon.

He stepped toward her and then bent, reaching out his hand to Amber. "Hold your shirt together and let me help you up."

She still trembled from the aftermath of being attacked, but she knew Desmon wasn't going to hurt her. It had been nearly fifteen years since they'd seen each other, but she was still fairly confident she was safe, at least physically. She wasn't sure about the rest of it.

She fisted her shirt together and reached for Desmon.

His hand was large and very warm as he gently pulled her up. Her legs shook, and her knees were weak, but she managed to stand. The second she did, she had to tilt her head all the way back to take in Desmon, and she quickly realized a few things.

He was taller and more muscular than she remembered.

Werewolves apparently aged very well.

Desmon was still tanned and clean-shaven, but the strong, masculine angles to his face gave him a harder edge.

Amber backed away. If she thought she'd hardened her heart or believed she was over him, she realized now she'd been fooling herself for years. The pain remained as fresh as if the wound had just occurred.

"My mother is dying." It was the first excuse that popped into her head, and it was a true one. "I have to go, Des."

She took another step backward but before she could put more distance between them, Desmon grabbed her. He gripped her arms with his big calloused hands, holding her in place. Their gazes locked, and she couldn't miss the anger she saw there. He lifted his head, breaking eye contact to look at the people behind her.

"I want everyone to *get out*. Clear the bar." He glanced over to the bartender. "Close it down, Jake."

"Most of the wolves here are from Goodwin. The bar is neutral territory. It's truce land. I can't make them leave because you say so."

Desmon snarled.

Jake nodded, like that was all that needed to be said. "Everybody out, now. You heard the alpha. If you feel like fighting him to stay, be my guest!" He paused and looked back to Desmon hesitantly. "Can I at least go to my apartment upstairs?"

"Get out!" Desmon shouted in that low, inhuman voice.

Curiosity had Amber looking behind her, astonished as everyone in the bar grabbed their belongings and quickly dashed for the exits. In less than a minute, the last person rushed out the door. Desmon's grip on her arms tightened, drawing her attention back to him. She looked up at him with a strange combination of fear and longing.

Desmon had matured while she'd been gone.

She studied his strong cheekbones, one of which had a faint scar that wasn't there before. His lips were still full and sensual, but his black eyelashes appeared thicker than she remembered, and his eyes still haunted her. She could see the pain of the past mirrored in them, as if his soul had been ripped open right along with hers.

"I looked for you," he whispered. "I couldn't find you. Where have you been? Where did you go?"

Amber swallowed past the emotion still choking her. "Los Angeles. I went to live with my biological father."

Desmon closed his eyes. His hold on her eased but he didn't let go. He took a deep breath, then another, before he opened those amazing eyes, locking gazes with her once more.

"I thought your kind didn't mingle with humans." She forced herself to look away and glance around the bar. Then she turned back to him and sighed in defeat. "I figured as long as I stayed in town, we'd never run into each other."

"Things changed." A muscle in his jaw jumped, making it obvious he was clenching his teeth. Then he asked, "Why did you come back if you didn't want to see me?"

"My mother really is dying. The booze, drugs and chain-smoking finally caught up to her. Katie is my half-sister, and so is Bea. They called to tell me Mom only had a few days left to live. I drove here yesterday morning. As soon as she passes, we'll bury her, and I'll be gone again. I swore to never return, but I had no choice."

"Why did you leave me?"

His voice was still low and scratchy, rather than smooth and refined the way she remembered. Again, it sounded like something else had stolen it and was speaking for him. Amber realized it was his animal side talking, and something about that wrapped around her heart, making the pain almost physical because she couldn't ignore the raw agony she heard. It was too much, and everything in her wanted to run away from it.

"You know why." Amber tried to step back, but he tightened his hold on her. "I need to go." She felt tears sting her eyes "You look good, Des. I hope the years have been kind to you. I was hurt, but I always wished you a happy life." She tugged more firmly to pull out of his hold. "You have to let me go now."

His nose flared as he sniffed at her, making it obvious he really was more animal than man right then. "No."

"Yes." She arched an eyebrow at him. "Please release me. Right now."

"*No.*"

"Excuse me? You can't keep me here. There are human police who would have a very big issues with you kidnapping me. And I don't even know why you'd care, anyway," she snapped when anger quickly made its way past the shock and pain. "Let's be honest. We were stupid kids. We barely got to spend time with each other—and you made your choice."

"I had *no* choice." Anger tensed his handsome features. "They would have killed you. I did the only thing I could. I *protected* you. You promised to be my mate, and I kept you safe. That was my job. I did it and you left!"

Her heart broke a little more, because he sounded like he meant it.

Desmon really thought he'd done the right thing...so she'd have to remind him. "You gave me to someone else, and you walked off into the woods with another woman to have sex."

"I *pretended* to give you to my best friend, knowing he'd never touch you. He made sure you weren't injured, and he got you away from Albert." Desmon's hold on her arm loosened, but he didn't fully let go. "Were you hurt? Did he do anything but take you to safety?"

"He got me out of there, but no, he didn't touch me." She jerked hard on her arm, pulling it free from his grasped, and backed up. "You got two out of three right."

"Amber—"

"I can't forget or forgive. I'm not even sure I know how. It's not like I grew up with a lot of love and understanding. This is where we are now, Des. There's no going back, no fixing what happened. Do you have any idea how much it hurts me to look at you? You were the only good thing in my life." She spun around and forced tears back as she walked for the door. "I'm sorry. I know this isn't all your fault, but I can't do this."

"You're all I ever wanted!" he called out as she tried to get away. "It never made a difference that we were young when you promised yourself to me. I'm not human like you. I can't write it off. Weres don't just move on after they've found their mates, Angel. We mate for life."

She paused mid-step, stopping for one moment, but the hurt was too much. She walked away from the man/wolf who had once held her heart. "Goodbye, Des."

2

Memories followed Amber out the door of The Barn. That fateful day on Desmon's sixteenth birthday, when she'd been forced to walk miles through the woods to a place she wished she'd never seen.

Desmon's people had gathered by a large area near the river. Seeing the dozens of strangers made Amber feel safer at first, but she had been horribly wrong. A thirty-something, blond-haired man approached the three men forcing Amber through the woods. Despite his frown, he had a nice, handsome face. He wore a suit, although it looked out of place, considering where they were. Amber still locked her terrified gaze on him, silently searching for help.

"You stole a human?" The man stopped, his green gaze examining her face closely, before he eyed the strong grip two of the men had on her arms. "What is this, entertainment? We don't need a missing person's report filed. It'll send law enforcement trampling all around our territory hunting for her."

The one who'd drooled on her earlier said, "We followed Des to her. He spoke to her. She left clothes out for him that she buried after he left them behind. It was obvious they do this often."

Shock crossed the older man's features, and his gaze turned icy as he studied Amber. "How do you know Desmon?"

She wasn't sure how to answer. She would do anything to protect Desmon, and he told her his kind didn't mingle with humans. He made it clear their friendship was a big no-no in his world, so she kept her lips firmly sealed together and decided she wouldn't talk.

"Perhaps you've lost your touch, Martin." The man stepped closer and sniffed her neck. "She doesn't scent of him."

"We're aware. If he were just him fucking one of them, we wouldn't have brought her to you, but that's not the case." Martin, the jerk who continued to grip her arm painfully, shrugged. "We thought you might want to find out what's going on, Alpha Albert."

"I do." Albert nodded, and then glared at Amber. "Speak now. Tell me what your association is with Desmon."

"I was walking in the woods," she lied. "I found clothes on the ground, and a bag. I just put them in it figuring someone had lost them. The road is right there, so I assumed someone accidentally left them." She prayed the lie would work and purposely messed up the name. "I don't know anyone named Desmond."

"You know Desmon." The older man's eyes narrowed, and a soft growl came from deep in the back of his throat.

"I don't," she denied.

"Get the hell away from her!" Desmon's voice rang out loudly, more of a snarl than actual words.

Amber looked over and watched Desmon storm right toward her. He was bare chested and bare foot, wearing only jeans. His entire body was tight with obvious fury. The jerk holding her gasped and released her, backing quickly away, despite Desmon only being a teenager.

In seconds, Desmon grabbed her and shoved her behind him. He reached back and wrapped one arm around her, holding Amber to him.

"Who is the girl?"

"She's my future mate, Alpha." Desmon's voice was low and gravely. "She's no threat to us. She's known about me since we were children and she's never betrayed my trust."

"Mate?" Albert laughed loud, a harsh sound that made fear shimmer down Amber's spine. "She's a sheep."

Desmon growled low and deep. "She's mine."

"I see." The alpha moved enough to peer at Amber past Desmon's shoulder. "Do you belong to him, human?"

She couldn't miss the way Desmon tensed as they all waited for her answer.

"Yes." She nodded and Desmon noticeably relaxed. So did she, since it was obvious she gave the right answer. "I do."

"Priceless." Albert's gaze turned icy cold as he fixed his attention on Desmon. "You broke pack laws by revealing yourself to one of them."

Desmon didn't hesitate or flinch. "I'll take my punishment."

Fear crept inside Amber, and she clutched at Desmon's jeans. The last thing she wanted was for him to get into trouble over her, but she just didn't know how to get them out of this mess.

"Yes, you will." Albert looked back to her and arched an eyebrow. "He'll take a beating with a whip for what he's done...unless you want to deny his claim on you. He'll take so many lashes, a human would drop dead halfway through it."

Horror washed through Amber and her mouth opened. Desmon looked back at her, his eyes wide as though telling her to stay silent.

"Don't say it," he ordered softly. "Trust me."

She didn't want him hurt, but she nodded and wrapped her arms around him, making it obvious Desmon's claim on her was valid.

Desmon faced his alpha once more.

"You have her trained well for a human." The alpha laughed harshly. "And I'm feeling generous since it is your birthday." He raised a hand. "Millia? Come forward."

Movement drew Amber's attention, and she watched a tall, lean woman in her early twenties walk out of the woods. Shock at the woman's naked body had Amber's eyes widening. Millia seemed oblivious to the fact she didn't have a stitch of clothing on in front of all these people. Dark haired and light eyed, her chin was held high as she moved with grace on long, beautiful legs until she reached them.

Albert caught Amber's stunned gaze. "She's beautiful, isn't she? She's in heat, and also happens to be my niece. I had planned to have Desmon fuck her and get her pregnant. Don't you think they'll make beautiful pups together? Strong little alpha pups to make our pack more powerful."

A snarl came from Desmon. "No, thank you, Alpha. I don't want her."

"I wasn't going to ask," the other man snarled back, rage gripping his features. "But things have changed. Millia complains she doesn't want a mate. Despite that, I'm offering her to you in exchange for your little human."

The dark-haired woman gasped. "Uncle, you promised I could just—"

"Silence," the man roared. His features changed and his eyes darkened. "I'm the alpha here, and I make the rules. Blood between us doesn't mean I'll take any lip from you. It'll be *you* taking the whip instead of Des."

The woman lowered her head quickly. "Of course. My apologies, Alpha."

"No," Desmon stated firmly. "Millia doesn't want me, and all I want is Amber. You'd be defying nature twice to force this. Thank you for the offer, but I have chosen my mate."

"So be it." The man smiled coldly, revealing sharp canine teeth that had extended down in his mouth. "I give you permission to mate her."

"Thank you, Alpha. She won't tell anyone about us." Desmon lowered his head like the woman had. "With your permission, I'll take her home. We greatly appreciate your blessing on our future mating when she comes of age."

"You'll do it *now*." The alpha's voice sharpened. "Today. I won't have a human running around putting us at risk. She's either a part of our pack or it's too dangerous to allow her to leave alive."

Desmon's head shot up, his body tense again, but then he nodded. "I'll take her home and do it immediately."

"No." The man smiled. "You'll do it here when everyone arrives. It'll be done in front of the entire pack." He pointed to the center of the clearing. "Right there and according to our traditions of old. You want to mate a human? She must prove to the rest us she's strong enough to be under my protection."

"Dad!" A new voice rang out. "Please don't do this."

The older man snarled, glaring at the blond teen who came forward. "Stay out of this, Jeremiah."

"I have known about her for years. On my word, she won't betray his trust."

"I'm the alpha." Rage gripped Albert's harsh features. "Not you. Not yet."

"Please." The younger blond stepped forward to stand next to Desmon, the two nearly touching shoulders. "He's a brother to me, and I ask this as a personal favor. Allow him to take her home and perform the mating his own way."

Albert removed his jacket and grabbed his nice dress shirt, tearing it from his body with one quick move. "You want a favor for him? Fine."

He glared at Desmon. "I'm giving you a choice, since my son has a soft spot where you're concerned. You either agree to the mating ceremony with your human right here, in the old traditional, or you can mount Millia to help her create a pup. You are of age now, and alphas are expected to stud for this pack. If you choose Millia, I'll allow you to give your human to my son. He can practice on your little sheep for his own studding obligations, since you both love humans so much.

"Let's see how brotherly you both feel toward each other then, knowing Jeramiah is going to fuck her. By handing her over, you're telling everyone in this pack you're giving up your claim to her forever. I'll personally make sure of it."

"Father," the blond choked. "Please."

"I've spoken," Albert snarled at Desmon , ignoring his son. "Make your decision now."

Amber wasn't sure what was going on, but she knew Desmon would mate her. His body trembled, and then he turned his head to stare down at her. She looked up into his eyes and saw pure fury burning bright in them, but then he met his friend's gaze.

"Protect her. I'm giving Amber to you."

It felt as though her heart stopped in her chest, and then in the next instant, her heartbeat roared in her ears. Shock ripped through her, but just as quickly, the agony of reality was forced on her when Desmon jerked out of her hold.

Jerimiah cursed. He grabbed Amber, yanking her close to his chest and pinning her in the cage of his arms. She fought the handsome, muscular blond, but his hold was like steel.

Jeramiah snarled at his father. "I won't forget this."

"Nor will I." His father laughed. "This has gone far better than I ever imagined."

Mute, and still reeling from Desmon giving her to his friend, she stared in disbelief as he stormed toward the naked woman, grabbed her hand and nearly dragged her into the darkening woods.

"Des?" Her mouth finally worked, and when it did, she screamed. "DES!"

He kept walking, not even sparing her a glance as he and Millia disappeared into the woods. Jeramiah cursed another blue streak. He said words even her step-father wouldn't, before he lifted Amber right off her feet, storming away in the opposite direction.

No matter how hard she tried, Amber couldn't shake off the memories of the past as she crossed the parking lot of the bar. Her hands shook as she unlocked her car door and wretched it open.

"Ams?"

She froze, her spine stiffening at the sound of Desmon behind her. She didn't have to turn her head to know he was close. She hadn't heard him follow her out, but then, she'd been in another time and place in her mind, reliving a nightmare she wished he would let her forget.

"You don't understand what really happened that day. At least let me explain, you owe me that."

Amber slowly turned to face the man she'd once loved more than anything. "This is too much for me to handle right now and I need to go. My mother could be dying as we speak."

She spun around and tried to climb into her car.

He reached out and gripped her arm once more. "Give me a few minutes to explain what happened so you really understand."

"No." She refused to look at him and jerked on her arm, but he didn't release it. "I'm sorry, but I have to go."

"Damn it." His tone turned into a snarl. "You're going to hear me out!"

Amber gasped when he spun her and pinned her to the back passenger door. He spread his bare feet apart to lower his height and held her forearms with his large hands. She jerked her gaze up when he softly snarled. His face changed, and no matter how good she'd believed her memory was, seeing his features shift into a more animalistic appearance scared her. She hadn't remembered him looking that terrifying when he'd done it in his teens.

"You're losing your face, Des."

"I don't give a damn." He released her arms and instead placed his hands against the car on either side of her to keep Amber trapped. "You belong to me...and *with* me."

"You gave me away, remember? You gave up that right. *You* broke the promise, not me. Now let me go."

His jaw seemed to lengthen, and sharp teeth grew out enough to be extremely noticeable. Amber's terror level notched up to high and she pushed back against the car, but there was nowhere for her to go

"Don't look at me that way. I'd never hurt you."

"That's a lie," she reminded him. "You already have."

His snout dropped, and he closed his eyes. He took deep, slow breaths, and then gazed at her again. She openly gawked at his features. A fine sheen of black hair covered his entire face and he resembled something straight out of a horror movie. Half human and half werewolf.

"I wanted you to see me this way, so you'd understand why I couldn't mate with you that night. Do you remember what that bastard said? He demanded I mate you in the middle of the clearing in front of all of my people. You don't even know what mating consists of, do you? It's not like a human wedding, Ams."

An uncomfortable feeling had her frowning. "At the time, I didn't know what to expect, but I've had a lot of time to think about it. He wanted us to have sex in front of everyone, right?"

"Yes."

Inwardly, Amber winced. "It would have been really awkward and horrible to lose my virginity in front of a crowd, but I could have survived it somehow with you. If you think sparing me that trauma hurt me less than you fucking someone else after pushing me off on your friend, think again. Can I leave now?"

Desmon leaned in, staring into her eyes. "He demanded I mate you in the *traditional* way. Look at me."

She did, unable to stop staring at his transformed features. "So? You look scary, but you used to lose your face sometimes when you got mad, and I wasn't afraid of you."

"Look at my body, Angel."

She hated hearing his pet name for her. It brought back painful memories of when they'd been happy together.

She hesitated, and then lowered her attention. Thicker hair covered his arms. It covered the surface where skin had once been, trailing down to his wrists. He lifted one hand, showing her the vicious-looking claws that stood out inches from his fingertips.

Amber ran her stunned gaze from them to his face again.

"Now let me share the ancient, barbaric traditions of my people with you. The woman would be stripped naked and staked down on her hands and knees in the middle of a clearing, to make sure all could witness the mating."

His voice deepened into a snarl. "The alpha would then have to approve the female by fucking her first. While that's happening, the relatives of the male mate would be holding him back, so he didn't attack the alpha for mounting his woman. Enrage a male werewolf and this is what you get, only feral and out of his fucking mind with jealousy and fury.

"If he approved, the alpha would leave, and the male would be brought to the female to complete the mating. The scent of another man on you would have driven me even more insane. My wolf would be desperate to rid you of his scent. I would have been brutal without meaning to. *That's* how he wanted to initiate you into our pack as my mate—if you survived."

Amber's knees gave way and she started to slide down the side of the car, but Desmon suddenly changed back to completely human. He grabbed her with claw-free hands around her waist to hoist her back up. He leaned in, pinned her to the car again, and his voice softened.

"He would have raped you in front of me, Angel. And I would have been helpless to stop him. He probably would have killed you, and even if you'd lived, I would have truly been insane at that point. I wouldn't have been in my skin when I reached you." He caressed her hips softly, like he needed the touch. "I wouldn't have been gentle. I would have taken you in that half-shifted state. It would have been brutal, and then I would have bitten into you to seal our bond."

She saw sincerity in his eyes, and her stomach heaved at the images he'd created. He nodded as he slipped his hands to her back, still rubbing her gently, as if the thought alone was enough to have him trying to soothe her.

"I believed you wouldn't survive, and I loved you too much to *ever* allow someone to rape you. The only way I could keep you safe was to give you to Jazz. I knew he would protect you, and get you to safety without anyone hurting you. I had no choice."

"Who's Jazz?"

"Jeramiah, but he goes by Jazz now. He changed his name after his father killed the human he loved."

Amber stared at his chest, unable to look into his eyes. The picture he'd painted had been enough to make her understand.

"Your people are truly fucked up." She didn't even feel bad telling him that as she looked back up at him. "Let me go."

Surprise flickered across his handsome face. "I was protecting you."

"I heard them inside. You're the alpha now, right? You're in charge?"

He gave a sharp nod. "I killed Albert for what he did to us."

"Oh God." She needed to get away from him. "You're a murder? That's what you've turned into?"

"I *did* kill him, and I won't apologize for protecting my people from that vicious monster."

"My mother is dying. Please move. I need to get to her." Amber looked up at him and pleaded, "Don't take this from me too, Des. Don't hurt me this way, by making me miss her last moments."

"I understand. I never wanted to take anything from you." Desmon jerked away as if the action physically hurt him. "But I'm asking you not to leave town." He gave her an intense glare, as if he were used to his commands behind obeyed with a simple look of warning. "We're not done talking."

She pulled opened the door once he stepped back. Her hands shook as she collapsed into the car. His words sounded threatening, and she refused to look at him as she drove away.

3

_____

*A*mber sipped coffee and stared at her sleeping sisters. Bea had passed out on the sofa, and Katie on the love seat. Exhaustion had Amber yawning but too many things were on her mind for her to rest.

Their mother had hung in there through the night, and then passed peacefully in her drug-induced sleep just past noon. The hospice nurse had been amazing, making all the tough calls. A doctor arrived shortly after, pronounced the death, and then the mortician showed up to take their mother's body away.

Amber had cried with her sisters, fixed them something to eat and talked them into at least lying down since they had stayed up all night and into the next afternoon.

There were still funeral arrangements to make, phone calls to place. She glanced at the clock. It was past five, so plans would have to wait until tomorrow. It was at least a short list of notifications. Dianna, their mother, had burned a lot of bridges marrying her second husband. Most of her family and friends had stopped talking to her. She'd chosen an abusive drunk over the people who'd cared about her.

It still made Amber angry.

Her mother had sided with that bastard against her own daughter. Memories haunted her of her horrible childhood. Rich had resented being stuck with her. He'd never tried to be a father to a child that wasn't his, calling her the shit end of the stick of a package deal. She'd always gotten blamed for everything and he liked to hit —a lot.

Her mother had just told her to try to do better, try harder, promising that eventually he'd come around, but he never had. Amber ran away after what happened with Desmon.

She put the mug down when her hands began to tremble. He looked good. Part of her had hoped he'd grown up ugly, but mostly she'd just wanted to avoid him. Luck hadn't been on her side.

She stared at Katie, worried. What was she doing hanging out with werewolves? Amber planned to have a long talk with her sister about Merl. Part of her even felt responsible. As the oldest, she'd let them down by not being around to look out for them and give them advice. Her loyalty to Desmon, and determination to keep his secret, had left her sisters vulnerable.

Memories of her marriage came next, and she snorted. It wasn't as if she'd lived a stellar life with Jeff and could claim to be a good example in the romance department. He'd been self-centered, controlling and manipulative. She should have known she couldn't trust him, considering he crafted creative lies for judges and juries on a regular basis to get his clients not-guilty verdicts. He'd been charming though, and she'd wanted the perfect life he'd presented to her. She'd had a nice home, money and the stability that came with it.

Amber stood and stretched, before walking around the house she grew up in. It had always been a dump, but the years had brought more neglect. Now their mother was gone, and someone needed to step up, especially since Bea wouldn't legally be an adult for another six months. Katie had made it clear she wanted to take care of their youngest sister, but that was before Amber learned she hung out in rough bars and dated a crazy, mean werewolf. A chill ran down her spine.

Decisions needed to be made. Tough ones.

"Why are you standing there glaring at the tub? What'd it do to you?"

She spun, staring at Katie leaning against the bathroom door. Her sister yawned, like the drama in the bar hadn't happened the night before, but Amber didn't let that stop her.

"You both should move to L.A. with me. We could sell this place and you two could split the money, whatever we can get for it, and put it in a savings account. I'll send you to college. I won't make you spend your inheritance on it."

"I'm not leaving."

"I'm offering you real security. That guy you're seeing, Merl, he's dangerous."

"You don't know anything about him." Katie spun, walking down the short hallway. "I'm going to bed."

"I *do* know." Amber went after her. She grabbed her sister's shoulder and spun her. "He's a werewolf. A bad one. That's enough."

"He's not that way normally. You pissed him off. You maced a werewolf, of course he overreacted." Katie jerked free. "This is basic shit when dealing with shifters, Amber."

"Now you're making excuses? Painting your own little fantasy that makes it okay, like Mom did with Rich? How many nights did you spend outside in the woods hiding or locked inside your room, while he knocked her around?"

"What do you care? You left."

It hurt, but Amber couldn't deny it. "He never hit you or Bea. I wouldn't have gone if he had."

"You left a long time ago, and things changed. Merl protects me. Nobody fucks with me anymore. Dad was harassing me for money after he left us, and he slapped me around when I told him I didn't have anything to give him. Merl made him stop."

"Who protects you from *Merl*?"

"He's never hurt me. He's a wolf, they're playful, but he knows the line." Katie sounded sincere, then she narrowed her eyes in suspicion. "How do you know Desmon?"

Amber looked away from her. "It's a long story."

"And you don't do long, do you, Amber? When are you leaving? Today? Tomorrow?"

"After the funeral. But I want you both to come with me this time. I have a three-bedroom condo. You'll like it. There's more than enough room for all of us."

"Pass." Katie stalked into her room. "Just leave, Amber."

Amber followed. "I want a better life for you, and I promise Merl isn't it. This house is going to fall down one day, and I don't want you to be inside it when it does. What about Bea? Don't you want a better life for *her*? Or does Merl have a friend you plan to set her up with? Is that your version of looking out for her? What's your long-term plan?"

Katie faced her. "Survival. It's what we do. One day at a time, big sis. You don't live here anymore. You have no idea how it is."

"And I'm offering you something better!"

"How do you know Desmon?" Katie repeated, rather than deal with the larger issue.

Realizing her sister wouldn't let it drop, Amber admitted, "I met him when I was a little girl. He was out running in the woods and a car hit him. He changed in front of me, and I hid him from Rich."

Katie plopped down on her bed like she was ready for a story. "That's against the rules. Letting humans know about them."

"How did *you* find out about werewolves?"

"I got a job in Hardly. They have a skin bar. Don't give me that look. I made great tips, and they didn't check my ID to prove I was old enough to serve beer. They just cared that I looked good in a bra and tight cutoff shorts. Dad had left. Not that he ever brought in much money, but we had nothing after he was gone. The only time he stopped by was to raid the house for more shit to sell.

"We were starving, and the electricity was about to get cut off. I had to work, and I needed more than what a fast food job paid. Then some dickhead got fixated on me and wouldn't take no for an answer. He scared the shit out of me. Turns out he was from another pack called Goodwin. You think Nightwind pack is bad?" Katie shook her head. "Des would kill one of his pack for raping a woman, but Goodwin doesn't have rules like that. Their males just take what they want.

"I had to quit my job, but that son of a bitch came after me, tracked me here and found me in our town while I was picking up groceries. I ran, got to my car, but he chased me in his truck. I made it about two miles out of town and saw cars parked across the road ahead of me. I slammed on my brakes, but I was trapped between them and that bastard in his truck. I thought my life was over...but they saved me. Merl, Jazz and Jason were the ones who'd blocked the road. The guy didn't take off, but instead tried to pull me out of my car. They all shifted and fought, killing the bastard. Des arrived and made me promise to never tell anyone what had happened or anything about them shifting. It was an easy promise to make. They saved my ass. I started dating Merl after that."

"I'm happy he saved you, but Merl really is trouble, Katie."

"He keeps my dad away and gives me money when I need it. Don't judge."

"Yeah, but what is he taking from you in return? He was going to fuck you in that bar in front of everyone."

She shrugged. "They're more comfortable with sex and nudity than we are. It's not a big deal to them, and nobody else ever tries to touch me. Merl would hurt them. I belong to him, and they respect that."

"You only belong to yourself."

"So, Des is protective of you because you helped him when he got hit by a car and kept my dad from finding him while he was hurt?"

Amber knew Katie was changing the subject again, but she'd made her point. "He used to come visit me out in the woods after that day. We grew close." It hurt saying the words. "He even asked me to be his mate when we were teenagers, and I said yes."

Katie paled. "That's a big deal to them, Amber. I'm not kidding. What happened? Why did you leave him? Alpha Desmon scares me a little, but he eats, sleeps and bleeds for the pack. Not to mention, he's *so* hot. He'd be a good one to come home to."

"Maybe he would have, but he broke my heart before I could find out. That's when I took off. I'm sorry I left you and Bea. I was young, and it was a stupid, selfish thing to do. I really thought you'd be okay, and I wasn't even sure if my father would take me in. I hitchhiked to L.A. and knocked on his apartment door. I was very happy to discover he still cared."

"How nice for you. It got hellish around here once the child support your father used to send stopped coming. He had you, so no more checks. Bet you didn't think of how pissed my dad would be over losing that booze money."

"No, I didn't," Amber admitted. "I was almost an adult anyway."

"Yeah, well, I'm not surprised. Don't come in here and tell us how to live. You lost that right a long time ago. Bea and I will be fine. Merl will see to it. I called him to let him know Mom died."

"You're better off without him. Come to L.A. with me." When that didn't work, Amber pleaded, "At least let me take Bea with me. She doesn't need to be exposed to him. What if she pisses him off, and he does to her what he tried to do to me?"

"Bea is *my* sister. Not yours. I'm the one who's been here for her all her life. Now get out of my room."

Amber was too tired to argue, so she spun and left, returning to the living room. Her baby sister still slept.

No way was she going to leave Bea in Hollow Mountain with Merl. Katie wasn't thinking straight. The guy had anger *and* spontaneous hair growth issues.

The sound of an engine drew her to the front window, and she pulled the curtain aside. A large gray truck parked on part of the lawn and Merl climbed out of the lifted vehicle.

"Shit." She walked to the door and opened it. She eased outside quietly and met him before he came up the porch. "I want to talk to you."

He curled his upper lip but stopped walking. "My alpha said hands off you. I'm still pissed about what you did to me, but I'm willing to let it go. I came for Katie."

"You're mated to her?"

"Fuck no."

He didn't seem the type to make a lifelong commitment, so she wasn't surprised. "I don't want you near either one of my sisters."

"I don't give a fuck." He stepped around her and headed toward the house. "Katie belongs to me."

She lunged and gripped his arm, then released him when he spun too quickly for a human and glared at her.

"How much money will it cost me to get you to leave Katie alone? I'm not rich, but how about five grand?"

He arched an eyebrow. "I'm not giving up Katie."

"My sister isn't your property. You admitted she's not your mate. Do you at least love her?"

"She amuses me, and she's good in bed."

She had to give him credit for honesty. "Ten grand."

"You're something else." He growled low. "Be glad my alpha put you under his protection, or I'd just kill you. Never stand between me and something that's mine."

"Twenty." It would hurt, but she was willing to pay it. He could dump Katie and her sister would agree to leave with her, getting Bea out of town with them.

He turned his head, openly staring at her car. "What about that? Would you sign it over to me?"

She inwardly cringed. She loved her Benz, but getting rid of it to save her sisters wasn't a tough choice. "Yes."

"Pass." He grinned, staring into her eyes. "I just wanted to see how far you'd go. Katie told me all about her older sister. You abandoned them to your drunken parents. I'd call you a bitch, but that'd be too much of a compliment."

"Rich wasn't my father, and our mother didn't drink when I left."

"That doesn't matter. Katie has a lot of resentment." He leaned in close and smiled. "Do you know what that means?"

"You're a low-life willing to take advantage of her?" Amber guessed.

He chuckled, not even bothering to deny it. "She appreciates belonging to me, and knows I won't give her up. That kind of loyalty and devotion is priceless." He turned away, jogged up the porch and entered the house before he added, "And sexy."

"Damn," Amber muttered, because he wasn't as stupid as he looked.

She followed him inside. He wasn't in the living room and thankfully he hadn't woken Bea. She continued to sleep on the sofa. Soft voices drew Amber down the hallway to Katie's bedroom. She paused at the partially open doorway, listening.

"No more excuses. I want you to move back in with me."

"I can't, Merl. I have Bea to think about."

"She'll be fine by herself. You can check on her."

"The social worker would be all over my ass. She's already come over here half a dozen times once hospice got involved for my mom. We talked about this. The state would come in, take custody of Bea since she's still underage, and sell the house to pay for her care if I'm not here living with her."

"That's bullshit. We'll sell the house now, so they can't."

"What about Bea?"

"She can live in one of my guest rooms."

"I don't think that's a good idea." Katie sounded firm. "I don't trust some of your friends not to mess with her."

"Are you arguing with me?" Merl snarled. "I've been damn patient with you since you moved home a month ago. I've had to cook my own meals and my place is a mess. What's the point of having you if you don't do anything for me, huh? I can't fuck you when I want anymore, and you don't take care of me the way you should. I deserve better."

"I know. I'm sorry, Merl."

"You should be. You need to be reminded that I'm in charge. You've gotten really mouthy since you've been staying here."

Amber had had enough. She pushed the door open a bit to peer in, prepared to argue with the jerk. Instead, she watched as Merl grabbed her sister, kissing her. Katie struggled for a second but then went limp in his beefy arms.

Merl ripped her sister's shirt, tearing it open to grope her breast.

"Get your hands off her!" Amber lunged forward and grabbed him from behind.

He jerked hard, and she stumbled back, tripped on something and landed on her butt.

Merl twisted his head, glaring at her. "Get your ass up and get out, or I'll hurt you regardless of Desmon's order."

"You should leave, Merl." Katie pulled her shirt together. "My mom *just* died, and you're being too cruel. I can't take this right now."

Merl turned on her. "What'd you say to me?"

"Just leave." Katie sniffed. "Please? We all need to calm down."

"You don't talk to me like that." He grabbed Katie by her throat and yanked her against his body. "I'm going to fuck you into submission again."

Katie fought, using her fists to punch at his face.

Amber didn't think, wanting to protect her sister. She kicked him in the back of his knee. It caused his leg to give out from under him, and he came crashing down on top of her. He didn't release Katie when he fell.

Amber tried to wiggle out from underneath Merl and her sister's tangled bodies, pinning her to the unforgiving hardwood floor. Katie kept hitting him and landed some good punches to the big brute. He howled out and rolled over. Amber got a good look at his face when he did, blood was pouring from his nose and his split lip.

He began to climb up Amber's body, trying to get out of the small space their bodies were trapped in.

Warm wetness hit her face, going in her open mouth, the blood almost choking her. She twisted her head, squeezing her eyes closed, and shoved at him but he was too heavy. She remained trapped under him until he got himself clear. Amber rolled onto her stomach, frantically trying to wipe off his blood. She opened her eyes in time to see Merl leave the bedroom.

"Fuck it. I'll replace you, Katie. Let your asshole sister take care of you from now on. I don't need this shit! I'm not getting killed by my alpha over a piece of ass. It wasn't even that good anymore." The front door slammed hard as he stormed out of the house.

LAURANN DOHNER & KELE MOON

Amber turned her head, locating Katie sitting up against the wall. Katie was crying, with blood on her hands. "Are you okay?"

"I hate you!" Katie drew her legs up and curled into an upright fetal position. "Why couldn't you just leave us the hell alone? I'm sorry we even told you to come home. You've ruined everything!"

"Amber!" Bea froze in the doorway, openly gawking at both sisters. "You're both bleeding! Should I call 9-1-1?"

"I'm okay," Amber tried to assure her. "This blood isn't mine. Katie? Are you hurt?"

"I've lost him." Katie began to sob. "I love him."

"I should call an ambulance." Bea appeared horrified as she stepped closer to Amber and helped her to her feet. "You've got blood all over you. It's in your hair and all over your face. He probably just gave you some disease. You'll need a shot or something."

"Oh my fucking God," Katie sniffed. "Merl can't carry diseases. Just get out of my room and leave me alone!"

Amber wasn't sure what to do. Katie began to sob again, and Bea looked terrified, confused and ready to burst into tears. "Everything is going to be fine." She wasn't sure what else to say, but she tried. "We'll figure everything out. Nobody's life is ruined."

"Come on." Bea tugged on Amber's arms. "We need to wash that blood off."

It was a good plan. Amber nodded and took a few steps.

Then she was struck by a heat flash like nothing she'd ever experienced before, and she froze. Her skin began to tingle too, all over her body. "What the hell? I feel like I'm having an allergic reaction to something."

"What's wrong?" Bea sounded alarmed.

"Shit!" Katie stopped crying. "Did you swallow some of his blood?"

Amber met her sister's tear-filled gaze. "I think so."

"And he had a hard-on. Fuck! Arguments turn Merl on." Katie climbed to her feet and wiped her tears, smearing blood on her face from her hands. "Bea, get her into a cold shower. It's bloodlust. Male wolves can put women into heat if they swallow enough of their blood."

"What does that mean?" Amber wasn't sure she wanted to know either.

"You just got dosed with Merl's hormones. He was horny. Guess what *you're* going to be for the next few hours? He sometimes gives me a little of his blood if I'm not really in the mood. It makes for super-hot sex—unless you've got an overbearing older sister who decides to stick her nose where it doesn't belong. Then it's called justice. He's never going to take me back."

Amber held still, trying to take in that information. She felt like she was running a fever now and her skin still tingled. It was actually getting stronger.

Then she stared into Bea's eyes, worried. Katie had said "male wolves." Amber hoped her baby sister hadn't heard that part or just assumed they were talking about real wolves.

She looked back at Katie. "Watch what you say."

"She knows." Katie picked up a shirt, wiping her hands on it, then used the material to rub her face.

"Shut up, Katie. You're going to get us into trouble," Bea warned.

Katie threw down the shirt. "*She* knows, too. Werewolves live in Hollow Mountain. Guess who has a history with Alpha Desmon?" Katie pointed at Amber. "It seems she not only left *us*, but she fucked *him* over, too. Now get out of my room!"

Bea led Amber into the hallway and to the bathroom. "You shouldn't have come back here if you're in trouble with Desmon." She turned on the shower, adjusting the temperature, and wrung her hands. "He's really nice, and helps us out even though we're human, but I wouldn't want him mad at *me*."

"You know him?"

"Yeah. Katie had some guy stalking her, and then she started dating Merl." She lowered her voice and drew closer. "Desmon gave me his phone number and told me to call him if anyone ever tries to hurt me. He knows I don't like Merl much. He was also worried that some of the wolves Merl hangs with might notice me, you know? He told me to stay away from them." Heat crept into her cheeks. "I've never had a boyfriend. I enjoy reading a lot and don't go out much. Katie and I are polar opposites, and I think he noticed, or he can smell it or something." Her cheeks grew pink, before she changed the subject and asked, "What did you do to make Desmon mad at you?"

Amber began to strip out of her clothes. "We grew up together, and kind of dated as teenagers. Then he broke my heart and I left. I don't know if you can understand this, but I couldn't stay here to watch him be with someone else."

"He was your one true love, wasn't he? You should see the pain in your eyes right now."

"It's because I feel miserable." Amber climbed over the tub lip and got into the shower. The water was lukewarm, but she couldn't stop shivering. Desperate to lighten the mood, she joked, "I think that jerk our sister is dating gave me werewolf cooties."

Bea didn't laugh. She chewed on her bottom lip, looking worried instead. "I hope you aren't going to turn into one of them. Do you know how they become werewolves?"

"No. You heard what Katie said. It's just bloodlust, whatever the hell that means. I'm sure I'll be fine."

Amber tipped her head back. She reached up to scrub at her face, letting the spray run through her long blonde hair, getting all the blood off. One glance down had her wincing. Red water pooled around her feet. The drain in the tub must have a small clog.

"You should come to L.A. with me, Bea. I think you'd love it there. I actually live a few blocks away from a large three-story library. You said you do a lot of reading." She turned her head to gauge Bea's reaction.

Her baby sister was gone, the bathroom door left open.

Amber shivered again. It was tempting to turn the hot water up but as she touched her forehead, it felt really hot. "Great. I have a fever."

Strange hot and cold chills wracked her body as she washed her hair and by the time she turned off the water, her teeth were chattering. She got out of the shower and dried off, then made her way to her old bedroom that had been turned into a guest room. She lay down on the bed and curled into a ball wrapped in a towel. Her breasts ached, her stomach felt as though it was on fire, but she was still freezing.

Goddamn werewolves. I'm going to survive this.

She heard someone enter the room when the floor creaked, and she turned her head. Katie stood next to the bed looking calmer. "Hey."

"Hey," Amber whispered, still shivering.

"You look like hell." Katie sighed, and her shoulders slumped. "Don't worry, okay? You couldn't have been exposed to much of Merl's blood. We're too far out for any of the other males to smell you, so all you have to do is get through it. He walked out on me once after giving me blood when I pissed him off. He wanted to teach me a lesson. He's not so bad once you get to know him, but he has a temper. It might feel like you're going to die, but I promise it'll pass." Katie pulled the blanket over Amber, tucking it in. "Give it a night. You'll be good as new." She pushed some of Amber's wet hair back from her face. "Then you should climb into that fancy car of yours and get the hell out of here. Save yourself. Part of me always envied you."

Amber rolled toward her. "Why?"

"You got out of this shit town and away from our parents. Don't you think I ever dreamed about that, too? Only about a thousand times. I just couldn't leave Bea." Katie stroked more hair back from her face. "I remember how bad you had it. Dad used to hit you and say you were devil spawn. He's the one who put a wedge between us as sisters. He encouraged us to not get close to you."

"So, come with me. Let's try again."

Katie pulled her hand away and straightened. "No. I heard you in the bathroom. You left because you got your heart broken. I'm staying to keep mine in one piece. Right or wrong, I love Merl."

"Then, at least let me take Bea with me."

"She actually loves Hollow Mountain." Katie shrugged. "If you knew her, you'd know that, Amber. This place reminds her of a fairy tale. You'd break her heart if you took her away. She's living in a town with werewolves. She reads all those books that make it seem more magical than it is. In truth, they're like us, just trying to survive. A few are good, most are assholes, but she doesn't see it that way. She likes the fantasy, and she definitely won't want to leave. Making her tell you no would hurt her, and you may think I'm a bitch, but my heart can't take seeing that after losing mom. I'll work something out so she's safe. I always do."

Amber watched Katie leave the room and head toward her own bedroom. She curled back onto her side and fought tears. Her skin felt cold, but she was burning up inside. Her clit started to throb as if it had a heartbeat.

The timing couldn't be more fantastic.

Exactly how much shit did life expect her to deal with this week?

Her mother dying, seeing the ex-love of her life, and dealing with sister drama wasn't enough? Some weird werewolf blood thing had to be added to the list?

"Goddamn werewolves," she muttered.

4

*D*esmon ran his fingers over one of his suits but turned away, opening the second closet in his bedroom. He'd gone for a long run, but it hadn't done anything to calm the wolf inside him. He couldn't put on a tie when he felt so savage.

His Ams was back.

And she didn't want anything to do with him.

The look of betrayal in her gray eyes haunted him. He dressed in jeans and a t-shirt, and tried to ignore the hurt her expression caused.

Still feeling wild, he decided to look for food since he couldn't turn to Amber for help with his *real* hunger. He left his bedroom and walked down the stairs to the kitchen, ignoring everyone he passed in the pack house. He slammed things around as he heated himself up some leftovers.

"Who's the woman everyone's talking about from last night?"

Desmon turned off the flames under the pans and dumped his dinner onto a plate. Then he looked at his friend, holding Jazz's gaze for a long moment before he sighed and admitted, "Amber's back."

Jazz stared at him in stunned silence, and then walked over to the fridge and yanked it open. He took out two beers and jerked his head at the table before he finally spoke. "Sit, Des." He took a seat and twisted off both caps, placing one bottle in front of an empty seat next to him. "The only Amber who would make you lose your shit in front of the pack is *your* Amber. That's major. How did she know to find you at The Barn? You're never there that often. And why'd she pick now to show back up? Did she run into weres and ask about you?"

"She wasn't there looking for me, and who the hell is going to know about Nightwind outside Northern California? We're small for a reason," Desmon recognized he was growling. "Katie Baker was there with Merl. Guess who her older sister is?"

Jazz looked at him with wide eyes. "No fucking way."

"Same mother, different fathers. I had a chat with Merl late last night, and he filled me in. When I was a pup, I always met Amber in the woods so no one would see us together. I didn't dare follow her scent back home and risk drawing other weres into her territory. I'd glimpsed her stepfather on and off back then from a distance, but he'd moved out before Katie started dating Merl. I'd have connected them as family otherwise. Why didn't *you* know? You were the one who took her home that day. You've been to Katie's place to check on Bea."

"Amber freaked out pretty bad when I carried her out of our territory and refused to let me take her all the way home. I never knew how to handle crying women, especially not at that age. She was also cursing me out and threatening to kill me if I didn't let her go. I guess she assumed you giving her to me was real, and that I might try to fuck her. I tried to calm her, tried to explain, but she'd have none of it. I put her down, made her promise to go home, and she ran off. I hung around a bit to make sure she wouldn't try to double back, but I never saw her again."

"Fucking Albert. Bastard's dead and I *still* can't stop hating him," Des rasped. "He fucked up our lives so much."

"*You* hate him? Try being me for a day. I thought him being dead might lessen my anger, but nope. If I'd done it, there wouldn't have been a body left to bury." Jazz took a sip of his beer, completely unapologetic for the confession.

Desmon looked at him in concern. "I hope you don't say that to other wolves. I understand, but he was your father, and this is the modern fucking era. We don't eat wolves we kill. That's a bit much."

"We'll have to agree to disagree. I'm still pissed about that grave." Jazz took another drink of his beer. "Anyway, Katie's mom is dying, and Amber came back. Makes sense. Now what?"

"I'll let you know when I figure it out." Desmon took a seat and set his plate down with a thump. Who the hell was he to give Jazz shit about anything this week? "I take it I'm the talk of the pack? I lost my shit when I realized Merl had her pinned on the floor. I was already pissed that he'd do that a woman. I might have actually killed him if Amber wasn't lying there watching. I didn't want her to see me like that."

"Why are you here and not with her? I know you well, Des. You never got over her."

"Her mom is dying, and she wants nothing to do with me. What was I supposed to do?"

"Did you tell her that you didn't fuck Millia? That she was forced into that shit by my father? That the two of you refused to breed him a pup he could raise to be the son he always wanted? 'Cause it sure wasn't *me*. He told me I was a huge disappointment all the time. He always made sure I knew."

"Amber wasn't exactly in a mood to listen. She just wanted to get the hell away from me, and she made it very clear that we were over before she did."

"Since when has that stopped you? You're Desmon Nightwind." Jazz smiled. "You took over the pack stolen from *your* father when you were sixteen, and you've held it all this time. Nobody else has ever done that before."

"We did it together, Jazz."

His best friend's smile faltered. "I'd move heaven and hell if I thought it would bring Marcy back to me. Your Ams is alive, Des. She's not lost to you forever. I'd do anything to be in your place right now. I sure as hell wouldn't be sulking around the pack house. I'd be tracking my mate down to get her back. You could spend the rest of your life with her. I'm never going to have that. I can only hope there's an afterlife, and Marcy is there waiting for me."

It broke Desmon's heart. "I'm so sorry."

"You didn't kill Marcy. You took out the bastard who did it."

"You killed three of Albert's enforcers by yourself, and you were only sixteen, too." A part of Desmon did feel sorry about that grave. Albert hadn't deserved a resting place or a headstone. He had an example to set for the other wolves, but that didn't help Jazz with the raging, mourning wolf who'd lost his mate before she was even fully his. "You avenged her, Jazz."

"My father was a piece of shit who made both of us lose our mates because he looked down on humans. He used to call them sheep, remember?" The words sounded bitter on Jazz's tongue, full of hatred for a dead man. He shook his head and looked back to Desmon. "Eat that burnt shit you just cooked and go after Amber. She's alive, man. Don't lose her a second time."

Desmon's voice cracked when he admitted, "She hates me."

"So what? She's in town. Don't let her get away. You can remind her why she used to love you. Tell her the truth about Millia. That would probably go a long way."

"I don't want to hurt her more, and I know some of our pack isn't going to easily accept it if I take a human mate. It's not just about what I want anymore. I took responsibility for everyone and swore to always put their needs first."

"And you're doing a fantastic job. Your father held this pack with a mate who used to be human, and the pack was happy. You can, too."

"Yeah, look how *that* turned out."

"My father was always nuts, Des. I know that better than you do. I think he hated humans because your mother chose your dad over him. Albert loved her, if you can call sick obsession 'love.' He claimed my mother a week after your parents mated. He wanted everything your father had. It's why we were born so close in age.

"Nesso Nightwind had the woman Albert wanted, so my dad took a woman many considered even more beautiful than your mom. Your father was talking about having a child, so Albert knocked up *my* mother with me. It took him years to convince some wolves to help him kill your father. He couldn't do it on his own. Albert abused and tore this pack apart. You are a great alpha, Des. You'll be an even better one with the woman you love at your side."

Desmon's phone rang, and he dug it out of his back pocket, glanced at the screen, then accepted it.

"What's wrong, Katie?"

"Mom died."

"I'm so sorry." Desmon felt a pain in his chest not just for Amber, but for all three sisters. "I know how hard it is to lose a parent. I'm here to help, just as I would be for one of my own wolves."

"Speaking of that...Merl came over."

He tensed. "Are you okay? Did he start any shit?"

"No. I mean, we got into a fight, but that's normal. Only this time, I hit him a few times."

"Did he hit you back?"

Des would kill him if he had. He'd warned Merl about that many times. Werewolves were much stronger than humans. Merl's father had been heavily controlled by Albert, and Merl suffered as a pup much the way Jazz had. They had both been beaten and mentally abused for not measuring up to ridiculous expectations, but Merl hadn't handled it as well as Jazz. Desmon had tried to salvage him, make him a decent wolf, but he didn't trust Merl not to majorly fuck up.

"No. Of course not, he never actually hurts me," Katie cut into his thoughts. "The thing is...Amber doesn't get how it is with Merl and me. She got involved."

Desmon stood so fast, his chair crashed to the floor. Rage shot through him. "Did he hurt her?"

"No!" Katie quickly answered. "I think I broke Merl's nose, though. Amber attacked him from behind, not understanding that it's our version of foreplay sometimes. I have to show him I can stand up to him when he becomes too controlling, and it turns him on. So, he was bleeding, and Amber kind of tripped him or something. He accidently fell on her and she got covered in his blood."

"Fuck."

"Yeah. She got some in her mouth or nose. Probably her eyes too. He was turned on, as I said. Bea put Amber to bed but she's burning up with fever. It's bloodlust. It's my fault, and I swear it was an accident! Merl took off the second he could. He didn't hurt her at all. I was the one who made him bleed, and she's the one who rushed into my room and attacked him."

"I'm on my way."

"Don't hurt Merl. I'm only calling because she's my sister, and I realize you have a past with her. I thought you'd want to come help her out if she's in heat."

"I'll be there in a few minutes." He ended the call and shoved his phone back into his pocket.

Jazz stood. "I heard. Want me to track down Merl?"

"No. I'll get Amber's version first. Katie would lie for him, but I don't want to assume she is. I need to go."

"Get to Amber. I'll handle everything here."

"I'm taking your bike."

Jazz unclipped his keys. "Claim your mate, Des."

"No, I won't let it go that far." He shook his head, even if the wolf in him howled in protest. "I could never tie her to me without telling her first. It's a law for a reason. Plus, she'd hate me for it later."

"It worked out for Jason."

"Brandi is much more submissive. Amber had a rough life growing up and would consider it a betrayal she could never forgive if I bit her right now. She knows what it means."

"Well, she needs you now." Jazz shrugged. "So, I'd make it count, big wolf."

Jazz tossed his keys, and Desmon caught them deftly. He ran out of the kitchen, through the back door, and found Jazz's motorcycle parked behind a few cars in the long driveway. He climbed on and shoved the key in. The engine vibrated to life between his thighs a second later.

Amber needed him, and she was in bloodlust. He'd be there for her and get her through it.

A little guilt surfaced as his dick hardened. He didn't want to be hard for her, knowing she was likely miserable being in heat—but he was.

He sped all the way to the old house in the woods. He'd been there twice to speak to Katie and her sister about Merl. The silver car was the one that Amber had been driving when she'd left The Barn the night before. He parked next to it, turned off the engine on Jazz's motorcycle, and hurried up the front steps.

Katie jerked open the door before he could knock. "It wasn't Merl's fault. And I called you, didn't I? I wouldn't do that if he had done something bad."

"Fuck Merl." Desmon didn't give a damn about him at that moment. He pushed past Katie and inhaled. He picked up Amber's scent immediately and every muscle in his body tightened with need. He had to bite the inside of his cheek to stop himself from growling. Still, his voice was low as he told Katie, "Go somewhere, and take Bea with you."

"This is *my* house."

He gave her a look, knowing she understood what Amber's scent was doing to him.

"Fine. I think I have ten bucks so we can have an ice cream in town or something."

Desmon yanked out his wallet and pulled out a few twenties. "Eat real food, and take your time. I'm sorry about your mother, Katie." He'd almost forgotten that part. "I need to take care of Amber right now."

Katie accepted the cash and lifted her gaze. "Don't hurt her. Her divorce was pretty horrible. She's already dealt with one guy screwing her over."

Desmon had to lock his knees. "She was *married*?"

"Shit. Um, I'm going to grab Bea and leave." Katie fled into the kitchen.

Desmon clenched his teeth. It could be worse. At least Amber wasn't married anymore.

He followed her scent down a narrow hallway to an open door.

She lay on a small bed, her slim body curled into a ball under an old comforter with her back to him. He stepped inside and quietly closed the door.

One glance back at the knob irritated him. There wasn't a lock on it, and it terrified him, because he didn't want to know what he was capable of if another wolf tried to break in. Amber made him feel dangerous, and he would've preferred to have her in a place where he felt she was protected.

Instead, he bent, tearing off his shoes and socks.

A low whimper came from Amber. He could detect the faint scent of pain filling the room. Bloodlust could hurt if someone tried to fight their body's urges. She obviously was, which didn't surprise him. She had no way of knowing what to do.

He tore his t-shirt over his head and unfastened his jeans, shoving them down. His briefs went next. He hesitated, knowing humans probably weren't accustomed to naked male werewolves crawling into bed with them to help out with blood heat.

A female were would simply welcome the aid.

Desmon bent and removed his wallet from his abandoned clothes. He opened it and pulled out a roll of three condoms he always kept there. Then he stalked closer, crouched down next to the bed, and placed the condoms on the floor. "Ams?"

She jumped, startled, then turned her head. Tears shone in her gray eyes and she stared at him with a feverish look.

"Hi." Desmon reached out and brushed some of her damp blonde hair away from her face, seeing her forehead was beaded with sweat. "Katie called me," he whispered. "She told me what happened."

"Wow, she really *is* pissed at me."

"She said you jumped into a fight between her and Merl. He bled on you."

"So, you came to see me be miserable?"

"No. Never. I came to help you."

She rolled a little toward him and broke eye contact, staring at his chest instead. Her light eyes widened.

"I know you're suffering right now. An unplanned heat can be very painful without a partner. That's what male wolves can do when you're exposed to their blood. It's actually illegal in our world, to force our blood on women, but Katie said it was an accident."

She fumbled with the covers to free one arm and reached out to him. He held still as she lightly brushed her fingers against his chest. He lowered his chin, watching her trace the tattoo over his heart.

"It's...it looks exactly like the wolf I carved for you."

"I made it our pack symbol." He lifted up enough for her to see more of his chest, but not reveal he'd completely removed his clothes. The word "Nightwind" was inscribed under the wolf. "You might have left me, but I've always kept you with me."

Amber reacted as if his skin burned by yanking her hand back. "Don't do this to me, Des."

"Do what?"

"I feel like shit." She fisted her hand. "Just leave me alone. I can't fight you right now."

"Then don't. Let me help you."

"Katie called you to get even with me. Mission accomplished."

"She's worried about you."

"Right." Amber squeezed her eyes closed and turned her face away. "She thinks I've come to wreck her life and steal Bea from her. I didn't know Rich would start hitting them once I was gone. They were the only two people I ever saw him give a damn about." She sucked in a sharp breath and writhed under the covers. "Shit!"

"Stop fighting your body. It's making you anxious. Try to relax."

"I'm burning up inside, but I'm so cold! Maybe I have the flu."

He'd had enough. Talking wouldn't help her. Actions would. He gripped the comforter with both hands and lifted it, revealing she only wore a damp towel around her body. "No wonder. This has to go."

She struggled a little, trying to get away, but the bed wasn't big and the other side of it trapped her against a wall. He got ahold of the towel and tore it off her, tossing it on the floor behind him. He rose up, climbed onto the mattress with her and yanked Amber closer.

She stiffened in shock. "You're naked!"

He ignored the panic in her voice as he turned her to face him. "Cuddle up to me. I'll warm your skin."

"This turns you on?" She gave him a dirty look. "You're poking me in the thigh."

"*You* turn me on. You always have, and I'm not going to apologize for it." He adjusted her again. She wasn't in any condition to put up a fight as she made feeble attempts to push him away. He came down on top of her, making sure he didn't crush her with his weight. "Wrap around me."

She hesitated.

"Do you want to get warm and stop hurting? Do it."

She hugged him around his neck, then spread her thighs and curled them around his waist. She hugged the back of his legs with her calves. "You feel feverish, too."

"I run hotter than you. All shifters do. Can you trust me, Ams?"

"Nope. Not as far as I can throw you."

He laughed and captured her face with his hand, so she had no choice but to look at him. It put their mouths close together. "There's that bluntness I've missed so much. I'm not going to hurt you."

"You mean again?"

That killed his humor. "I didn't touch Millia. I walked off into the woods with her but that's *all* I did. She didn't want to have a baby with me. Her uncle ordered her to. Once we were alone, I told her I'd rather die than get her pregnant, and she said we had that in common. We lied to Albert by swearing we'd fucked, but it never happened. She ran away to another pack before her next heat cycle, so he couldn't order her to try again."

"She's gone?"

"She came back after Albert was killed. She mated the wolf she loved, and they have four pups. Her uncle had forbidden her from mating while he was alive because she fell for someone he didn't approve of."

"Enough." She shivered under him. "I don't know if you're telling me the truth or not."

"I wouldn't lie to you, Angel."

"Don't call me that. I don't know you anymore, Des. I'm not sure if I ever knew you."

"I don't have any pups. Ask your sisters if you don't believe me. Millia was in heat. If I had fucked her that night, I would probably have one." Desmon caressed her arm while trying to keep the inhuman growl out of his voice because she smelled like pure sex. "Let me help you."

"You are, actually. I'm warmer. I still feel like shit but I'm not shivering."

"It's not going to get any better until you find an outlet. You're suffering bloodlust, and it is agony without a partner."

"What does that mean? I don't want to kill someone. Just the thought of getting up and trying to walk makes me want to cry. I hurt all over."

"I can make it better. Will you trust me?" He searched her beautiful eyes, hoping she'd agree.

She didn't look convinced, but she nodded.

"Just go with your instincts and *don't* fight them."

He closed his eyes and did the one thing he'd always wanted to. He kissed his Ams.

She had a soft mouth, and she gasped, opening up to him. He took advantage of it and swept his tongue between her lips.

He expected her to try to twist away, but Amber surprised him when she kissed him back, opened–mouthed and hungry.

The rush of desire nearly blinded him.

He growled when he felt her small, firm breasts pressed against his chest. She dug her fingernails into his skin, pulling him closer. She even arched her back, frantically grinding her pussy against his lower stomach, making him near savage with lust. He'd told her not to fight her instincts, and his angel had listened.

He released her face and ran his hand down her side to cup her ass. She had a great one that perfectly filled his palm.

Amber traced a hand up from his shoulders and fisted his hair at the back of his neck, as if she were afraid he'd stop kissing her. *Hell hasn't frozen over yet.* She ran her other hand down his arm, and then tried to wiggle her fingers between their stomachs. She moaned against his tongue, kissing him with a frenzy that matched his own. He lifted his hips a little to allow her to reach her pussy, assuming she wanted to rub her clit. Most women were mindless for pleasure when consumed with bloodlust.

She bypassed herself to find his hard shaft, and he groaned when she wrapped her fingers around him. She tried to pull him toward her pussy, bucking a little to bring them closer together, since their bodies weren't quite lined up right.

He ignored the pulling on his hair when he turned his head enough to free his mouth. "Condom first."

"Des! *Now*, I hurt!"

He opened his eyes and stared into hers, realizing the moment she gave into the bloodlust, it had consumed her.

"One second. I brought condoms." He tried to lean a little to the left to reach where he'd left them on the floor.

She viciously yanked on his hair to keep him in place and lifted her head, going for his throat like one of his kind might. He groaned when she bit him. It wasn't hard enough to break skin, but her hot, wet mouth and those teeth did a number on him. His dick was rock hard, and his balls ached to the point that he could barely think straight. He wanted to be inside her as much as she wanted him there.

"Condom," he snarled, trying to remind them both that they needed one.

"It's okay," she panted under him. "I got it."

It was nearly impossible to think with the scent of her arousal filling his nose. It had grown so thick in the small room that he could damn near taste how wet and needy she'd become. His lower belly, where she still rubbed her pussy, was proof enough she was ready to take him.

Amber bit him harder and stroked his shaft, bucking under him with a greedy desperation that was forcing his wolf to the surface whether Desmon wanted him there or not.

He lowered his hips, trapping her arm between them, and letting his weight settle over her in an attempt to pin her down. She was surprisingly strong for a human, likely from the bloodlust. He leaned to the left again but Amber clung to him, so she turned with him as he blindly reached over the side of the bed, trying to find the damn packets.

The shift of their bodies freed her from being completely under him, and she let go of his hair to hook her arm around his shoulder. She arched her hips right as he brushed the roll of condoms with his fingers. He couldn't get a good hold on them since they slid on the hardwood floor. He scooted more to the left, and Amber squeezed him, guiding the crown of his shaft to her pussy.

He froze, closing his eyes as she rolled her hips.

"Fuck," he snarled.

She was wet and hot. It was torture as she adjusted his dick just a bit and tried to use her grip around his hips to pull him closer with her legs. She was small, tight, but so ready to take him. She gasped loudly and rolled her hips again, still holding his dick, trying to guide it into her.

"Condom," he got out again.

"Dés, I got it. I'm on the shot. I can't get pregnant." She bit him again, moaning his name against his skin. "Please!"

He wasn't a hundred percent certain human birth control would work, but his hold on the beast slipped and he jerked his arm up, braced his elbow on the bed, and shoved his body to the right, centering over her. "Let go," he ordered.

Fuck knew, he didn't want a stupid piece of latex between them when he finally took his mate.

It had been so damn long, wanting her—needing her—desperately.

She released his shaft and pulled her hand out from between them, groping his ass instead. He thrust forward slowly and threw his head back as he sank his dick into the snug confines of his Ams.

His wolf went insane, and he almost howled.

They were intimately joined, the way he'd fantasized about

forever, and it was better than he'd ever imagined by a thousand times.

Amber moaned and bucked under him. He'd told her to follow her instincts, so he did the same. He pinned her under him tightly and began to thrust, fucking his mate hard and fast. Everything inside Desmon demanded that he make Amber his and show her that she belonged to him.

Her sharp cries and moans helped him figure out exactly what pleased her the most. Every hard thrust pushed her closer, and she climaxed quickly, her body tensing beneath his with a shuddering gasp of ecstasy. She clung to him tighter, her nails digging into his shoulders, her vaginal muscles squeezing his dick so tightly, he couldn't hold back—he came too.

Violently.

A whitewash of pleasure that made his teeth grow long, but Desmon was still there somewhere. He turned his head rather than bite her, even if everything in him was screaming at him to finally tie Amber to him forever.

5

Amber clung to Desmon until her breathing slowed. She kept her eyes closed, with her face buried against his throat. They'd just had sex...and it had blown her mind. Parts of her body below her belly button felt a little short-circuited too, in the best way. They were practically plastered together, with her wrapped around his big body, and his cock still inside her. She'd always wondered what sex would be like between them.

Now she knew.

Desmon seemed determined to destroy her. Seeing him again had been hard enough. All she'd wanted was to leave town before she could make a fool of herself a second time. It had been difficult enough to pick up the pieces of her broken heart the last time Desmon hurt her. She'd worked hard at moving on, had married Jeff, then survived an ugly divorce.

Desmon made her feel more in one night than Jeff had throughout the entire course of their marriage. It wasn't just with her heart, either. Now he'd shown her he could do it to her body, too.

He adjusted his weight over her a little as he slid his fingers into her hair. He gave a gentle tug but she refused to move. He might want to talk, and she had nothing to say. Not yet.

"Angel," he rasped. "Are you okay? Was I too rough?"

She shook her head.

"Look at me."

"No."

He tried to lift his upper body away from hers, but she tightened her arms around him. He quickly stopped and held still. "What's wrong?"

"Just hold me, Des."

"I am. I'm never going to let you go, Ams. You're mine forever."

That's what she was afraid of.

He had her pinned on the old mattress, and it felt so right being under him, as if she belonged there. That was the worst thing of all. The differences between them were even more severe than they once had been. She used to dream that they'd live some happy life together, but life with Jeff had taught her the downfall of being with a man in a powerful position. It came with a lot of responsibilities and drawbacks.

"You lead your pack now, right?"

"I do. Albert can never come between us again."

"How many people depend on you?"

He didn't answer right away. "It doesn't matter."

"I was married."

"I heard." His entire body stiffened over hers. "You're divorced now, correct?"

She almost flinched, hearing his harsh tone. "Yes. He was a lawyer, owned his own firm, and was very wealthy. He fought me tooth and nail after I left him."

"He didn't want to lose you. No one would."

"It wasn't that. It was about the money. I wasn't going to walk away without a dime. I put up with a lot of shit for the years we were married, and I deserved some compensation. I demanded a fourth of his net worth. He could keep all the business assets and houses, but I wanted a cash settlement. I fought him to get that."

"Why are you telling me this?" Desmon tugged her hair lightly once more. "Will you look at me?"

"No. Not yet. It's better if I say this while I can't see your face. I took a backseat in Jeff's world. He had to impress clients and life was always a production. You know, like a show. I always had to act as though I was happy, even when I wasn't. I had to dress a certain way, play the part of devoted wife. He ended up doing a lot of things that hurt me. When I confronted him, he said certain behaviors were expected of him. There's always a price to pay when you're with someone in a powerful position."

Desmon said nothing.

She tried to figure out how to get her point across. "I can't be with you, Des. I'm never going through that again. I don't know what it's going to cost me, but I'm sure it's too much. I'm already over my limit of pain that I've endured and survived."

"I'm not your ex."

She took a deep breath and blew it out, finally pulling her face back and turning her head. She stared into his beautiful blue eyes. "You said you don't have to sleep with women who want to mate your men, but what other painful things will I face? I'm not like you. I know your kind doesn't think much of humans. We're sheep."

"Albert thought that way. I don't. You *know* I don't."

"What about the people you lead? Who's to say they won't hate me?"

"They won't. One of my enforcers just took a human mate, and they're very happy. She doesn't want him to change her, but our pack accepts Brandi as she is."

"How many other women are you going to sleep with to keep up appearances or whatever?"

"What?" His eyes widened, making him look truly horrified. "None."

"Bullshit. You're powerful, if you're running your pack. My ex kept mistresses. He told me I should have expected it. Powerful men need them to impress others. And let's not even talk about what happened at The Barn with Merl."

"I'm not your ex," he reminded her once more. "That bastard cheated on you?"

"He got one of them pregnant. That's how I found out. A process server showed up at our house during a dinner party. The guy stated why Jeff was being sued, loud enough for everyone to hear. Otherwise, I probably wouldn't have found out it was to establish paternity. He'd dumped that mistress when she'd refused to get an abortion, so she went after him for child support."

"What kind of asshole did you marry?"

"A big one." She adjusted her arms and lightly gripped the curve of Desmon's shoulders. "I didn't know what I'd be dealing with when I married Jeff. I was naive and stupid. What's the price of being with *you*, Des?"

"We get to be together and happy." All the anger slipped away from his features. "I'd never hurt you, Angel."

She shook her head. "We're too different."

"You've always known what I am."

"Actually, you never really answered much about that. I don't know anything about your culture, aside from it being extremely screwed up. I still have nightmares about your sixteenth birthday."

"So do I." He flinched as though talking about it hurt him. "Things are different now. Not perfect, but I'm working on it. Albert really fucked up my pack. He hurt a lot of us by twisting the rules. Like the mating thing. He said it was old tradition for the alpha to take the female first, but he just wanted to fuck every woman he could. He used any excuse he could get."

"Didn't he have a mate?"

"He did for eight years, but she was in a bad car accident. Albert found her. She'd lost control in the rain and slammed head-on into a boulder. Wolves are tough, and we heal from a lot of things a human couldn't survive. It's a good thing, too, because it's impossible to take our kind to a hospital. Our blood work isn't right, you know? Anyway...Albert had killed our only pack doctor in a rage. Her injuries were too severe to heal from on her own, and she died. After that, he tried to nail any woman who caught his eye."

"I'm glad he's dead," she admitted. "Maybe he won't show up in my nightmares anymore, now that I know that."

"I would kill him all over again if it would undo what he did to us," Desmon whispered, his voice more of a growl. "And your ex-husband better stay away. You were mine, and he didn't just steal you from me—he hurt you."

"I'm not yours. I already told you I can't do that," she reminded him, but the impact was sort of lost because he was still buried deep inside her. More so, his cock remained hard and thick. When she tried to pull away, Amber ended up biting her lip instead to hide the moan because she was still so hyper-sensitive from whatever the bloodlust was doing to her. "God, Des."

"Tonight you *are* mine, Angel." Desmon thrust against her, making her choke back another gasp. "And I'm going to make sure you know I'm not your ex-husband. I've had too much taken away from me in my life—I cherish what's mine. Even if it's only for one night."

He wrapped both of his large hands over her wrists. Then he took her harder, making her cry out and arch into him because the lust hadn't been eased the way she'd thought. If anything, it was more intense as he licked down the line of her neck, and then bit lightly at her shoulder with teeth that felt sharper than they should be.

"You feel so fucking good. If you agreed to be my mate, I'd want to live inside you just like this."

It was so easy to believe Desmon when he was moving inside her. She found herself wrapping her legs tighter around him as he kept her pinned to the bed, forcing her to feel the bliss of the hard, firm strokes of his cock. Her pussy clenched as she instinctively fought for release, even though she had just come.

She turned her head, letting him lick and nip at her neck, her shoulder, her collarbone, a few of his love bites on the edge of painful, but somehow it only heightened the pleasure.

"I want to claim you," he growled, this time sounding more wolf-like than human. "You have no idea what it's taking to hold myself back, Ams."

She bowed beneath him when the ecstasy slammed into her, and screamed as it started pulsing through her system. It was too intense to fight as it rolled over her, wave after wave that seemed to grow stronger rather than wane like usual. She tossed her head against the pillow, breathless, lost in the release, but she still heard Desmon let out a low, animalistic growl.

His hips started pumping against hers harder, faster, until he stiffened over her. It felt as though his cock grew inside her, extending her pleasure, but it was difficult to tell when everything was hazed in bliss.

When he let her go, she wrapped her arms around him, holding him when she should be pushing him away. It had been such a hard year, and for one night, she needed this fantasy. She wanted to touch the dreams of her youth, even if she would surely wake up in the morning and know it was a mistake.

Desmon held Amber rather than pull out of her as he rolled to his side and took Amber with him. He brushed her hair away from her face and studied her features with that amazing light gaze of his, then he sighed. "I can't fix it all. I can't change the past. The only thing I can do is enjoy you tonight. All night. Tomorrow, we'll deal with the rest."

Amber was starting to realize Desmon was the boss of his people for a reason. What he said made sense. When he spoke, a part of her wanted to believe him, even if it left her wide open to being hurt again.

In the morning, she could sensible. Tonight, she just wanted to enjoy Desmon and forget the rest.

6
_____

*a*mber awoke to the smell of cooking bacon and brewing coffee. The scent was warm and homey in a way she wished she could associate with her childhood, but couldn't.

Her body was achy, and she rolled over on the small bed, burying her face in the sheets. She could still smell Desmon there, just slightly, that spicy, masculine scent of his that she knew wasn't store bought.

It was just him.

The combination was very appealing, like a hazy dream of someone else's life that was a little too perfect, but no less compelling because of it. Amber knew not to trust it. She'd been married to a rich man. Her entire existence had revolved around making sure everything appeared picture-perfect. Enviable.

The big house.

The luxury cars.

The designer clothes.

All to paint a picture of perfection that was nothing but a mask that hid the stress and misery. Power had always been so much more important than humanity or kindness to her ex-husband. He was willing to step on anyone, including Amber, to hold on to that image and keep others impressed and intimidated.

Never again.

Amber tried really hard to steel herself against believing the dream as she dug her robe out of her suitcase and tied it on. The ache between her thighs was noticeable. She just wished she didn't enjoy it as much as she did.

She'd never felt so thoroughly well-fucked before.

Desmon wore her out to the point that, hours later, she was still exhausted. It was nice, like the smell of bacon in the air and the tinge of alpha male on her sheets. It didn't matter, it was temporary, a way to touch the past for one night—now they were back to reality.

Except, it was Desmon standing in the kitchen, shirtless and barefoot in only jeans. He was cooking, both Katie and Bea already sitting at the counter, eating breakfast.

To their credit, neither of them spoke, but Katie's smirk and Bea's blush said it all. Since they were all aware of what happened the night before, Amber decided to ignore the elephant in the room and ask Desmon, "What's this?"

He looked at the bacon in the pan. "Sometimes us wolves eat in the morning. We call it breakfast. I thought you might enjoy the tradition."

"Funny," she said dryly.

"I'll dish you up some so you can try it." Desmon put two strips of bacon on a plate, and then reached for the pan with scrambled eggs. "Do you want coffee?" He pointed to the coffee maker with the spatula in his hand. "Just tell me if I'm overwhelming you with our cultural differences all at once."

"I'll take coffee." She sat on the stool next to Bea, who was reading a book as she held a piece of bacon she was nibbling on. "I'll call the school for you and explain that Mom died."

"I enjoy going to school. It will keep my mind occupied. Besides, I have a Calculus test today." Bea gave her a wan smile, and then looked at her phone on the counter. "I'm going to be late." She leaned over and kissed Amber's cheek. "Love you."

Bea jumped up before Amber had the chance to say anything else. They hadn't been close in a long time, but it was obvious her youngest sister wanted that to change. Amber wanted it too —desperately.

Bea kissed Katie's cheek, too, and Katie grabbed her hand. "You want me to drive you?"

"No, I know you're late for work. I'll take the bus." Bea shouldered her backpack.

"I could drive you," Amber reminded her. "I have a car, too."

"No. Eat your breakfast." Bea grinned as her gaze darted to Desmon. "Bye, Des."

"Bye, Bea." Desmon put eggs on Amber's plate as Bea walked into the living room. "Hey, listen, I want you to stay on pack land the next few weeks. A lot of wolves saw what happened at the bar. That could make any of you a target. I know you have school, and our enforcer's watch the bus routes, but after that, keep near home. All of you stay close." Desmon looked to Amber with an arch of his eyebrow. "That means you, too. Promise me, Ams. If you're going to drive Bea to school, let me know."

"Sure," Amber agreed as she took a sip of coffee, knowing it was for protection, more than control, that he wanted to know where she was going.

"Yeah, we'll stay close," Bea agreed, and then hit Katie's arm. "We *all* will."

Katie shrugged in agreement. "I don't have any money to go out anyway."

"I have to take off." Bea gestured to the door.

Desmon waved her off with the spatula. "Learn lots of important things."

"Always," Bea promised, and the front door slammed behind her.

They all sat in companionable silence after Bea left.

Desmon gave Amber her breakfast and she ate, surprised at how good it was. "I'm impressed," she had to admit to Desmon, who stood by the sink eating the food he'd plated for himself. "Given the chance, my ex-husband could burn water."

"I already told you, I'm not your ex-husband." There was a slight growl to Desmon's voice. "And judging from last night, I bet I have *lots* of skills he doesn't."

Amber couldn't believe he'd just said that, and she looked to Katie, who dipped her head to hide her grin. "You think that's amusing?"

Katie shook her head, but her smile betrayed her. Then her gaze darted to Desmon, like that was enough to keep her silent. That just irritated Amber more. Even in this cozy, domestic breakfast scene Desmon was trying to paint, his power was obvious.

"You should call in to work," Amber told her sister, rather than give in to the bait. They couldn't hide from reality forever. "I want to make sure your wishes are honored when we start handling the funeral arrangements for Mom, and I'm sure your boss will understand."

"Yeah, but my bank account won't. We're poor, Amber. Not sure if you know what that's like anymore, but I can't take off. Not if I want to keep Bea from starving," Katie said bitterly.

"We would never let you and Bea starve, Katie," Desmon cut in before Amber could say anything. "Are you having a hard time buying food? I noticed your fridge was close to empty."

"I'll buy my sisters food," Amber snapped at him. "You don't get to just come in here and take over because of last night."

"He was helping us before you got here. *You're* the one who's taking over." Katie jumped off the stool. "Alpha Desmon offered us a pack plot at the cemetery when I found out Mom was dying, and he already started making the arrangements this morning. That's what he does. He takes care of people. Maybe he'll teach *you* how...before you leave again."

"I sent Mom money." Amber was shaking when she realized how difficult it had been for her sisters. "I sent her fifteen hundred dollars a month from the moment I married Jeff."

"Then I guess they drank it." Katie grabbed her purse off the counter and walked out of the kitchen without a backward glance. "'Cause we never saw it."

Amber sat there after the front door slammed and Katie left her alone with Desmon. Her cheeks were hot with embarrassment, fury and sadness. She hated that he had a front row seat to not only their sibling meltdown, but her failure as a sister.

"Death is hard on families." Desmon sighed. "Don't be mad at her, Ams. It's so easy to get angry. To be bitter. It's hard to be young and have so much responsibility."

"I know. She has a right to be bitter." She held a hand out toward the door. "But she makes me feel like every problem in her life is my fault."

"I wasn't talking about her, actually. I don't know if she's bitter or not." Desmon flinched when he said it. "But I do understand some of what Katie is going through, and I wouldn't blame her if she was."

"Right." Amber dropped her hand when she realized he was talking about himself. "How old were you when you became alpha?"

"Sixteen."

She frowned. "But—"

"I never recovered from what Albert did to me. I know I keep saying this, but a commitment to mate is very different for wolves than it is for humans. My primal side felt as if he'd stole my mate from me. After everything else I'd already endured because of him, my wolf constantly lurked right under the surface, angry, waiting for the right opportunity to strike. Unfortunately, Albert was a bigger asshole than we anticipated. I could've saved lives if I had killed him the night he chased you away. I could've spared Jazz."

"Jazz?" she frowned.

"Jeramiah. My friend who took you home that night."

"Did he kill his own son?" Amber gasped in horror.

"No." Desmon shook his head. "Jazz is still alive. He holds the pack with me. We're co-alphas. It's unusual now that we're older, but at the time, we were both young wolves. We needed each other to lean on. Plus, we were both dealing with similar loss."

Amber was scared to ask, but she did anyway. "What'd that asshole do to him?"

"It's a sad story, Amber. You have your own wounds to heal from." He glanced at her plate. "You're not eating your breakfast."

Amber took a bite of her eggs, and then looked at him expectantly. "Tell me."

"We had a human girl who lived in our pack. Jazz was close with Marcy. Sort of like you and me, they weren't mated yet, but it didn't make a difference to Jazz. She was his, and he was waiting until she reached maturity to claim her."

"Where is she?" Amber whispered.

"She's gone." Desmon's voice cracked when he said it. "A few months after you left, Albert had her killed rather than risk his son being mated to a human. We never found her body, just smelled her blood where she was attacked. Jazz couldn't even bury her."

"How do you know she's really dead?" Amber argued. "There had to be a body."

Desmon shook his head. "It wasn't uncommon for there to be very few remains left. Especially when wolves like Albert are in charge."

"Oh my God." Amber's stomach lurched when she realized what he was saying. Over the years, she'd tried not to think of Desmon's friend because she had so many of her own terrible memories associated with him, but never once could she deny that the handsome blond werewolf had been kind to her. "Your poor friend. How did he handle it?"

Desmon was quiet for a moment before he said, "Not very well. Jazz killed the enforcers who smelled of Marcy's blood—*all* of them. I had to kill Albert, or I would've been forced to watch him execute his own son for the crime. My only regret was that I waited so long. Like I said, I should've done it the day he brought you to pack land. Right there, in front everyone—including my mate." He looked at her as he said it. "I should've ended it then. I'll spend the rest of my life being haunted by the mistake."

Amber had her own massive set of issues about that night, but she couldn't deny the horrible pain Desmon had suffered, either. "You were so young, Des. You can't blame yourself."

"Sure, I can." He pointed at her plate. "You're still not eating."

She took a bite because he had taken the time to cook for her, and that was an extremely rare, almost non-existent occurrence in her life. A silence descended on them, but it was a comfortable one. When she was done, Desmon took her plate and started washing the dishes.

He could not possibly be that amazing in bed *and* do dishes, but the proof was in front of her.

"If you don't want to use one of our plots for your mother, I understand," he said with his back to her. "I don't want you to think I'm overstepping my boundaries in your family."

"No, you didn't know they were my family when you offered. That was very kind, Des," she had to admit. "We'd be happy to accept the plot."

"Okay." He turned back to her, those light eyes intense and contemplative. "Would you like help making arrangements today? Most of being an alpha is actually business related. Dealing with humans. Solving problems. Paperwork. Boring stuff most wolves hate, but I do alright with it."

Warning bells were going off everywhere in Amber's mind, but her sensible side was forced to wage a terrible battle with her heart. She wasn't just horribly saddened by his story. She was touched by Desmon's deep loyalty not only to his friend Jazz, but to her sisters as well.

"Please," she decided when her heart won the war. "I'd love help."

When Desmon said he was good at handling business, he wasn't kidding. He took care of everything surrounding their mother's funeral, but he was considerate the whole time. He dealt with the funeral home director when the greedy man tried to overcharge them, but let Amber, Katie and Bea sit down and discuss little things like music choices for the service.

When Amber went to sign the papers for the bill, it said there was a zero balance, and she automatically looked to Desmon, who simply smiled. "Turns out your mother had a small insurance policy that handled the costs."

"Oh." Amber looked back to the papers again, knowing for a fact her mother would never think that far ahead.

"Wow, that was really thoughtful of her," Bea whispered from the seat next Amber.

"Yeah, I can't believe it," Katie agreed. "Maybe she gave a shit after all."

Amber glanced back to Desmon once more, but rather than argue, she sighed. "Maybe we'll use the money I was going to spend for something else then."

So they picked out music, and had the funeral director make up memorial programs for a funeral few would attend using insurance money Amber was certain didn't exist. Afterwards, Desmon took them home to give Amber and her sisters some time alone.

Three days later, Amber was well prepared for the three of them to be sitting there with only Desmon in attendance, since her mother didn't have many friends, but something surprising happened.

People started showing up.

Desmon's best friend Jazz arrived looking like a very tall, extremely buff blond model in a black suit. Behind him was another man, equally tall, with dark hair and olive skin like Desmon. He seemed uncomfortable in his suit as he draped one muscular arm around a short, curvy woman with long, curly brown hair who wore a beautiful black dress.

"Katie." Jazz hugged Amber's sister. "I'm so sorry."

"Thank you, Alpha." Katie's voice sounded choked as she said it, and then she let go of Jazz, and hugged the man next to him. "Jason, thank you for coming."

"Of course." Jason returned her hug. "You remember my mate Brandi."

"Yes, thank you for coming, Brandi." Katie hugged Jason's mate, clinging to the other woman, making it obvious to Amber she also hadn't expected anyone for their mother's funeral. "Really, thank you."

"You're not alone," Brandi assured her. "Not even close."

"Baby Bea." Jazz hugged Bea tightly. "How you holding up, little girl?"

"Better now." Bea sounded as relieved as Katie to have others there.

Brandi walked over to Amber, hugging her like a friend even though they were strangers. "I'm sorry for your loss."

Amber returned the hug, clinging to the shorter woman for being there, even if she didn't know her two seconds ago. "Thank you, Brandi."

"Brandi's human. She's the woman I told you was recently mated to one of my enforcers, Jason." Desmon gestured to Jason next to Brandi. "Jason, this is my," he paused, seeming to search for the right description, and finished with, "my Amber."

"Nice to meet you, Amber." Jason hugged her. "Sorry about your mom. I know how hard this is."

"Thank you." Amber nodded and turned to Jazz, who stood back rather than hug her, as if he wasn't sure she would want to be touched by him. So, she took the initiative and hugged the big blond. "Jazz, thank you."

Jazz seemed grateful, and he nearly crushed the air out of her when he returned the affection and whispered in her ear, "I'm sorry —for everything."

"Des explained things." Amber knew they weren't just talking about her mother. She thought about Jazz's mate, who'd died too young, and clung to him tighter. "I'm sorry, too."

Jazz released her, and she could tell by the look on his face that he understood what she was sorry about. The haunted glaze in his light eyes told her he was still in deep mourning over the girl he'd lost as a teenager.

Amber felt a little dazed as she turned toward the door, seeing others coming in. Muscular men who looked as uncomfortable as

Jason in their suits. Lithe, beautiful women wearing black dresses styled similar to Brandi's, and there were so many of them.

Amber turned to Desmon in shock. "Are they all werewolves?"

"Not all of them." Brandi smiled. "Roni's human, too." She gestured to a petite brunette with big brown eyes. "This is Roni. She works at the bar in town. The Barn."

Desmon tensed next to her, but Amber smiled. "I've been there. You have your hands full, Roni."

"True story." Roni leaned in and hugged her. "So sorry, Amber, but so glad to meet you. We need to become best gal pals, 'cause I heard what happened at The Barn, and I know a girl whose made of steel when I see her."

Amber just laughed. "I don't know about that, but I'm grateful to you for being here. All of you."

"We're not perfect, Ams." Desmon sighed. "But we take care of each other. We consider Katie and Bea pack. They all wanted to come to support them."

Amber glanced over to Katie, who was hugging another big, burly werewolf, and Bea, who clung to Roni like an old friend. "I believe that."

"You're pack, too." Desmon looked at her with that earnest, compelling blue gaze. "Most of them know who you are."

She frowned. "How?"

"I made no secret about losing the woman I considered my mate. Now you're back." Desmon shrugged. "And crazy as it sounds, most of them want their alpha to be happy."

"It doesn't sound crazy," Amber assured him as she watched more werewolves walk in and comfort her sisters. Like Desmon said, these wolves weren't perfect. There was a darkness to them that scared her, but there was good there, too, and she suspected it was Desmon who helped bring it out in them. "Not at all."

7

The next ten days after her mother passed were a blur.

Usually, Amber considered death somewhat isolating. No one wanted to hang around long enough for it to touch them, but the Nightwind werewolves weren't like that. The evening after the funeral, they started bringing food over. All sorts of food.

Some of it, Amber wasn't particularly excited about. The venison sausage and frozen rabbit burger patties seemed unappealing, but Katie and Bea ate them, making it apparent this wasn't the first time they'd received wild game gifts from the werewolves. Other dishes were amazing, like Jason's peach cobbler that his mate Brandi brought over. There were lots of frozen stews, soups, meat patties, and it was obvious the wolves didn't waste things and were used to stockpiling food.

Desmon explained that they did that in case hunting became scarce in the area. They mingled with humans now, but for a long time they hadn't.

"I don't know how your sisters eat those rabbit burgers," Brandi was saying as she leaned over the large deep freezer Jason had brought over in a truck. She wiped out the inside, her jean-covered ass high in the air as she kept complaining. "I love Jason, but I'm not eating frozen Thumper."

Amber suspected Katie and Bea learned to eat them because they'd been struggling for a long time, and any food was good when it was scarce. It angered her, wondering what their mother had done with the money she'd sent every month to help them out. It obviously hadn't gone to improving the house or helping to feed her sisters. That mystery would remain unsolved, since she couldn't ask a dead woman. Her best guess though, as Katie said, was it probably had been wasted on booze.

"Well, they eat them." Amber shrugged rather than explain.

"And now you have a place to store them. Glad Jason found this in the shed out back." Brandi leaned farther into the freezer, so much so her feet barely touched the ground because she was so short. "And you're doing me a favor taking the extra food, because all that frozen meat has been taking up too much room in our freezer. I think you're doing the whole pack a favor. I know Jason's not the only one with a meat-hording problem."

Jason came out the backdoor, making it obvious he heard them talking. He walked up behind Brandi, grabbed her hips and leaned over to nip at her neck. "You love my meat."

Brandi laughed and reached back, smacking his chest lightly.

Rather than be deterred, Jason just growled, low and animalistic, a sound no real human could make. He flashed dangerous canine teeth that had grown long. Then Amber saw him actually bite the curve of Brandi's neck. Not violently, but hard enough that two small specks of blood appeared on Brandi's pale skin. Jason licked at the tiny wounds, slowly, with a low grunt, as though her blood was the greatest thing in the world.

When Amber heard a growl behind her, she turned, seeing Desmon standing there watching them just as intensely as she was. He had stopped by this morning to help Jason, even though he was in alpha mode, complete with the designer suit and tie. His long dark hair was pulled back with a single black band, showing off his handsome face and strong jawline. He resembled a powerful businessman, but his light eyes were darker than usual, pupils dilated like those of a wolf, making him seem wild and almost feral.

"Jason." Desmon's voice was harsh, not quite human, and undeniably reprimanding.

Jason turned back to Desmon. His pupils were dilated the same way Desmon's were. Amber blushed to realize Jason was blatantly hard, his cock straining against the line of jeans, and he didn't seem self-conscious about it.

Jason looked confused, as if he wasn't certain what he'd done wrong. Still, he cleared his throat and mumbled, "Sorry, Des."

"They have no boundaries with it comes to sex." Brandi translated for Amber as she straightened up. Her face was flushed, her long, curly hair chaotic as she shoved it over her shoulders. Then she turned to Jason. "Humans call that PDA, public displays of affection, and most consider it rude." Brandi sighed and looked back to Amber. "Jason knows better, believe it not, but he forgets since we're around wolves all the time and none of them care."

"You're my mate," Jason stated, as if that should explain it all.

"We'll handle the freezer." Desmon's voice was still low with unbending authority. "Thank you again."

Amber knew the mate thing was a sensitive subject, but it was likely Jason and Brandi didn't. On the outside, Amber and Desmon were on good terms.

She'd decided to spend the money she would've used for her mother's funeral on the house her sisters refused to leave. Desmon had been there every day since the funeral, helping get the house ready for more elaborate repairs, and fixing the small things that didn't require a contractor. Desmon was surprisingly handy, and she was too thrifty not to accept the free help. To others, their rekindled relationship looked cozy, almost domestic. They didn't know Desmon hadn't touched her since the night Merl's blood put her in heat.

Amber was embarrassed when Jason and Brandi left quickly.

She wanted to snap at Desmon for being bossy, but she bit her tongue instead. He'd been so helpful, and she knew he had good reason to be grouchy. Truth was, she was growly too, because the sexual tension between them was slowly starting to drive her insane.

When he stepped closer to her, she realized something. This was the first time Desmon had been alone with her in nearly two weeks. There was always someone underfoot. Bea or Katie, or members of Desmon's pack, like Jason and Brandi, who showed up to help with the house or drop off food.

This morning, Bea was in school. Katie was at work. Desmon had just stopped by to help Jason move the freezer, though Amber was certain Jason could've gotten it off the truck on his own. She'd been watching the werewolves work for a while now and they were far stronger than humans.

Desmon was supposed to go to the pack office afterwards and do whatever it was alpha wolves did all day, but he didn't seem like he was interested in going anywhere. Instead, he stood there with his broad shoulders noticeably tense under the lines of his suit. His pupils were still dilated, making him look untamed and incredibly sexy in a way that Amber didn't want to admit she found exciting.

The rush of longing was blinding as it washed over her, making her almost ache with the need to peel that expensive suit off him and touch Desmon, even if it was just one more time before it all went to hell.

Desmon's nostrils flared, and he closed his eyes. He was completely still as he stood there, reminding her of an animal stalking prey. Something about his strong, powerful stance made her nervous. Even the expensive suit couldn't hide what he really was— not today.

Needing a distraction, Amber turned around and took up Brandi's abandoned chore of cleaning out the inside of the freezer. She knew she was being a coward, hiding in the task without saying anything or even acknowledging they were alone for the first time since that night.

For a long minute, Desmon let her work. The sound of his breathing echoed over the chirp of northern California birds. She tensed when she realized he was watching her, and she got the impression he couldn't stop himself from staring.

Desmon was as powerless to this crazy attraction as Amber.

Then he stepped forward, crowding into her personal space. Desmon gripped either side of the freezer with his big, tanned hands, trapping her. She stared at the way his knuckles strained, making her worry the edges of the freezer may crumple under his werewolf strength.

"I don't know if I told you this." Desmon breathed the words against the curve of her neck. It caused a shiver of pleasure to rush over her, making her nipples tighten and her clit ache to the point that she squeezed her legs together. Desmon took another deep breath, and his voice was husky when he confessed, "Wolves can smell desire."

Her cheeks heated for an entirely different reason, but the clash of embarrassment and yearning only made her hotter. It was obvious he knew it, because the growl that came from him was pure wolf, hard, animalistic and undeniably possessive. She wished she didn't find it so compelling, making her feel wanted and feminine, desired, when she had been alone for years. Long before her divorce, her bed felt very empty. Truthfully, she'd been feeling cold inside since the day she'd left Desmon behind as a teenager.

He ran his fingers up her arm, lightly, making all the fine hairs stand on end as he whispered in her ear, "Want help with that problem, Angel?"

She tried to hide the moan of longing, but she knew he heard it. Desmon touched her hip, caressing it through the material of her blue day dress as he made his case. "Just you and me. No bloodlust, only our natural chemistry, the way it was supposed to be all those years ago. Don't you want to taste it one more time?"

She closed her eyes as both her soul and body screamed, *God, yes.*

Desmon pushed the sleeve of her dress down her arm, exposing her shoulder, and then licked her bare skin with another low growl. It seemed he couldn't resist tasting her. She never agreed to his offer, but she also didn't stop him as Desmon started pressing hot, wet kisses against the curve of her neck, her shoulders, her nape. He forced the other sleeve of her dress down her arm like a man used to being in charge, taking what he wanted without apology, and it left her wound so tight that she stopped caring about what it meant to want a powerful man.

She just enjoyed it.

He kept kissing her hypersensitive skin, and she leaned forward, holding on to the freezer to keep herself steady. She was so wet, it was disconcerting knowing Desmon could smell the lust coming off her, but he didn't seem to mind. In fact, it was obvious he loved it as he traced one hand up her bare thigh, underneath her dress. Her breath caught when his touch trailed between her legs. He ran his thumb along the line of her pussy, teasing her through the thin cotton of her underwear.

Amber moaned and gave up lying to herself about this.

She dropped her head down, surrendering completely, and something about the action affected Desmon. He snarled, this time a low rumble of possessiveness as he slipped his hand inside her panties and felt for himself how turned-on she was.

He circled a finger over her clit. The shock of pleasure was electric, and she gasped. Then she reached behind her and pulled the band out of Desmon's hair. She fisted the silky strands rather than beg, holding his face in the curve of her neck as she spread her legs in a silent plea to get her off.

Desmon took the invitation and started touching her, soft and teasing, leaving Amber sweaty and weak-kneed while he traced small circles over her clit. He took her right to the edge as she gasped and moaned without shame, but then stopped before she could climax. Instead, his touch moved lower, down the line of her pussy, making her push her hips forward in invitation.

God, she wanted him. She was practically vibrating with the need to feel his hard, thick cock inside her.

She could feel his arousal against her lower back, and she knew he was hurting, too, so she gasped, "In me, Des."

"Not yet." He pressed a kiss against her nape. "You'll come harder if we let it build. You've been so stressed. Even if you won't say it, I can sense it. You need a slow release, and you know I won't be able to go slow once I'm in you again. Wolf's too close to the surface. It'll be better if you're relaxed, and I like hearing you. It's calming to me, knowing you're getting off on my fingers."

She moaned at the image his words created, but still she reminded him, "We're outside, and I know your people have *really* good hearing. They'll know what we're doing."

"Even better," Desmon said in that rough voice of his.

"That's an alpha wolf thing, I can tell."

"Yes, it is." He licked her neck, letting her feel the sharp points of his teeth that had grown long. "Be happy that's the worse of it."

"Why?" she pressed, even as he started circling her clit again with his fingers, making her breathless once more. She tossed her head back against his shoulder and pulled his hair because she couldn't help herself. "Tell me why, Des. What do you want to do to me right now?"

"I want to bite you," Desmon growled. "I want to taste you and fuck you and own you." He nipped at the soft spot at the base of her neck, letting her feel his deadly teeth once more. "And I want you to own me, too."

Something about the way he said made the pleasure burn brighter.

"Is this a mate thing? Is that part of it?" she rasped when he started rubbing her clit quicker, with just the right amount pressure to leave her gasping. "You want me to bite you? Like a wolf?"

"Fuck, yes," he groaned.

She wanted to at least find a way to think clearly, but her thoughts splintered under the pleasure.

"Don't stop this time," she pleaded, as everything in her fought for the orgasm. "God, Des, I need this."

He didn't stop.

He let the bliss build and build, until finally Amber cried out. She would've lost her footing if Desmon didn't tighten his other arm around her, leaving her surrounded by him. His strong arms. The spicy, wholly masculine scent that always clung to him. His warm breath against her neck that made her skin tingle as the ecstasy pulsed through her entire body. All the while, Desmon touched her, dragging out the climax for what seemed like forever.

She was embarrassingly weak in the aftermath, but she let him hold her rather than fight it. It left her feeling peaceful, which made her truly recognize the constant stress-coaster her life had been since she was a child. As foreign as it was to her, it was still nice to surrender, to let him be strong for her. For once, to feel safe and protected.

Desmon brushed Amber's hair off her sweaty neck and pressed soft kisses against her nape. She felt the hard outline of his cock against her lower back, but when Desmon let out a low, rumbly growl, she heard his contentment, too.

He needed to hold her as much as she needed to let him.

She could feel the soft points of his wolf teeth as he trailed his lips over to the curve of her neck. He nipped at the tender spot with another low groan. The longing coming off him was so potent she could almost taste it, and she reached back to caress his thigh through the fine material of his slacks. It reminded her how split Desmon's life really was. Man and beast, pain and power. Amber knew Desmon's life was all about his pack. All work, all the time. He didn't take much for himself—except this.

How much could one little bite really hurt?

"Just a taste?" she asked him softly. "It won't do anything? You won't change me or mate me?"

"You'd have to drink from me to change over completely, and more than just a taste. It takes a lot of blood to transform a human. A few drops can't do more than put you into heat for the night, the way it did before. As for the other, I'd have to be partially shifted and inside you to mate you, Ams. Then, if I bit you, you'd be mine." The longing was blatant in his voice. "If I bit you with my fangs, it'd just be a tease. You wouldn't change over. You wouldn't be tied to me. You can walk away when it's over." He licked her neck and groaned once more. "But I still like the tease. Fuck, you smell good. I bet you taste even better."

She wasn't sure if teasing him was more cruelty than anything, but still she said, "Do it."

And his low growl made the risk more than worth it as a fine sheen of desire danced over her skin. Instead of biting her, he licked her neck again. At the same time, he palmed her breast, making her moan from the fresh surge of desire that blossomed so easily for him.

Desmon kept kissing her neck as he ran his hand lower, over her hip, before his touch slipped beneath the lining of her panties once more. Instead of rubbing her clit, he pushed one thick finger deep inside her.

She gasped from the rush of pleasure. She was still so sensitive from the first orgasm, this was almost too much, but she gave into it anyway. She dropped her head and pushed her hips against his hand as he started stroking her deep. When he pushed in a second finger, she was lost, dripping wet, gasping, right on the edge of coming again in an embarrassingly short amount of time.

She reached behind and fisted his hair once more, holding his face in the curve of her neck, because as insane as it was, she *wanted* him to bite her. She was wound tight, waiting to feel the sting of his teeth piecing her flesh. The sharp edge of danger from Desmon made it hotter.

This wasn't the kind teen she'd fallen in love with all those years ago, this was a powerful, deadly werewolf who didn't just run in the pack—he led it.

Desmon kept touching her instead of biting, fucking Amber with his fingers until her entire body was shaking with the need to come. He growled—low and possessive.

That was her only warning.

Surprisingly, she barely noticed the tear of delicate flesh giving way to his razor—sharp canines. The tidal wave of ecstasy made it impossible. The rush was so all encompassing, she screamed under the force of it. He kept pushing his fingers in her over and over again as her pussy clenched to the pulse of her powerful orgasm.

Never in her life had she felt something even remotely close to that.

Every stress melted away.

All her fears evaporated.

The tiny voice in the back of her mind disappeared; the one that always reminded her she wasn't good enough to love. The same one that told her they all left eventually, anyone she trusted would betray her. Her mother. Her stepfather. Her ex-husband. Desmon. Maybe even her sisters, even if they didn't want to—they would turn their backs on Amber.

Right then, it all felt like a lie, because it was almost as though she could feel the love from Desmon. The possessiveness. The overwhelming need to keep her close and protected, it was like ambrosia to Amber, because she'd *never* felt safe. Maybe a few times when she was a teenager, spending time with Desmon in the woods, but those memories were all clouded now under the weight of betrayal.

Or maybe not.

It felt pure again.

She didn't want to trust that it was truly him she was feeling under the pulses of pleasure and emotion crashing over her—but what if it was?

What if there was a person in this world who wouldn't hurt her?

The first thing she noticed when it started to wane was the rough brush of Desmon's tongue against her neck. She realized he was licking the injury the way a dog would. It should have been strange, but it wasn't. It still felt like she was sensing him, the real Desmon beneath the suit and scary alpha wolf exterior. She could feel his insecurities, too, knowing the world had hurt him worse than even she'd endured, and Amber got the impression she was the only one he let see it.

For the first time, she felt the tenderness of the wound as he kept licking it, but she didn't care. She caressed his hair, and then slid her hand to his nape, wanting to both soothe him and keep him close at the same time.

"Des..." she whispered, but found she didn't have words for what she'd just experienced.

"No one's going to harm you, Ams. Not while I'm around." There was still a low growl to his voice, that carnal possessiveness obviously at the forefront. "I killed the last man who hurt you. *Never* forget that. It was your face in my mind when I finally ended Albert."

He was obviously feeling Amber as strongly as she felt him. He had somehow managed to taste all her fears, despite how deeply she sensed his need to shield her from them.

"I believe you," she choked, still overwhelmed with the emotion because trust didn't come easily to her.

"I would never hurt you." His breath was warm against her skin, and he licked her neck once more. "I was protecting you that night. I couldn't let Albert hurt you just to keep you for myself. I'd be alone forever before I risked your life."

And wolves weren't like humans.

They mated forever.

He wasn't able to move on the way she had tried to do.

Not that it had worked out any better for Amber.

She was still pondering it when Desmon suddenly stiffened behind her.

She craned her neck, seeing that he was looking toward the open sliding-glass door on the porch. Once again, he reminded her of a dog, tense and on alert, ready to attack the mailman or whatever poor individual was walking up the driveway, not knowing this house was guarded by a very territorial canine.

Desmon snarled, sounding scary in a way she had never heard from him before. Then he took off, running so quickly it was almost impossible for her mind to accept it.

No human could move that fast.

From the other room, she heard, "Fuck!" but it was shouted in the same type of low, inhuman voice.

Amber followed Desmon without fully thinking it through. If she were smart, she would've run the other way, knowing another werewolf had entered the house without permission.

Desmon obviously thought he was a threat.

She was still recovering from feeling him, and she knew he wasn't fully rational right now. All that hurt and betrayal was still looming between them, making him feel as vulnerable as she was.

She followed the echo of growls—and blinked at what she saw in the living room.

Jazz was in the corner next to the bookshelf, holding up his hands, white hair showing on his open palms. His face was partially transformed, too, likely on instinct, even though he was still clearly more human than Desmon.

"It's windy today. There's a lot of dust, and you know I'm not the best scenter to begin with," Jazz was explaining evenly, but his voice was completely inhuman. "I didn't smell it until I walked in. I'm not challenging you for her. I thought Jason would need help with the freezer. I didn't even know you were here. I walked in blind."

Desmon took another menacing step toward his best friend. Amber stared at him from behind, noticing that his broad shoulders were incredibly tense underneath his suit. The hands clenched at his sides were hairy like Jazz's, and she could only imagine what his face looked like.

Desmon growled again, and something about the threat must've rubbed Jazz the wrong way.

Amber remembered that he was an alpha wolf, too.

Jazz growled back, showing off canines that had grown long and dangerous. "Fine! Wanna fight me? Bring it!"

She screamed when Desmon jumped at him.

Jazz was obviously expecting it, because he dodged to the side so quickly, Desmon crashed into the wall. She didn't realize how dangerous their claws were until Jazz slashed at him, ripping Desmon's beautiful suit, and seriously pissing him off in the process.

Desmon snarled and fought back, grabbing Jazz's upper arm with one hand and lashing out with the other. There was suddenly blood everywhere as the two alpha wolves crashed into the coffee table. Neither one of them fully transformed into their wolf forms, probably because they were dressed, but it still reminded her of watching a vicious dog fight, with growls, snarls and the flash of deadly teeth.

It was hard to tell who was winning until Desmon pinned Jazz down and sank his teeth into Jazz's biceps in a completely different way than he'd bitten Amber. She covered her mouth with both hands to stop herself from screaming again when she saw the spray of blood after Desmon tore he teeth away, obviously trying to cause as much injury as possible.

It was hard to tell, but Jazz sounded as shocked as Amber when he growled and grabbed the wound on his arm. When he lifted his hand, looking at the blood dripping off his fingers, his light eyes were wide, as though he couldn't believe what he was seeing.

She wasn't sure how werewolves called uncle when the fight got too intense, but she was certain backhanding Desmon so hard that his head snapped to the side wasn't the wisest move on Jazz's part.

Desmon was completely unfazed by a blow that would probably kill a human. He just snarled again, flashing his teeth menacingly, and Amber was terrified the next bite would be to Jazz's jugular.

It wasn't as if Desmon hadn't killed an alpha wolf before.

"Stop it!" she shouted at the top of her lungs.

"Nah, kill me instead!" Jazz growled back at Desmon, showing off his teeth in the same threatening manner. "Kill me, big wolf! You want to kill your best friend? Do it! I dare you!"

Apparently, Jazz's survival skills sucked—badly.

"Desmon!" Amber's voice cracked with a fear she couldn't hide. "Please stop hurting him!"

Desmon turned to her, his pupils so dilated and wolfish she could barely see the rim of bright blue. His face was hairy and transformed. Blood still dripped off his lips.

So very different from the man who was touching her a few minutes ago, he looked like the thing horror movies were made of— but something changed in his gaze as he studied her. His pupils went back to normal, making him seem more human. Desmon crawled off Jazz and stood while studying her.

Jazz slid back and ended up in the corner of the living room again. He touched the open, gushing wound on his arm, and looked at his hand once more.

"You were going to kill me." The hair on Jazz's face started to recede. He went from primal to something else before their eyes as he whispered, "What if I'd been someone else?"

"He wouldn't have killed you." Amber winced, because the horror on Jazz's face was terrifying. She grabbed Desmon's hand and pulled him closer to her, farther away from Jazz. Then she stepped in front of him, using herself as a human barrier between the two alpha wolves. "You just had bad timing. He was feeling a little possessive because of what we were doing."

"A little possessive?" Jazz repeated, giving her a look of disbelief. "Any other wolf but me, and he would've ripped out their throat without meaning too. I'm not trying to be a dick, but you two *need* to mate. He's a hazard to our pack while you remain unmated."

"Jazz." Desmon's voice sounded less inhuman, a little saner, with the thread of guilt already finding its way past the insanity. "I know this was my mistake. I bit her. I still had her blood on my tongue when you walked in. I let the wolf get the better of me, but I won't let you make her feel forced into mating."

"You've mourned her all this time." Jazz looked to Amber. "Did he confess that yet? Has he told you that he's *never* recovered from losing you? He would be a good mate to you, Amber."

"I understand what you're saying...but I'm human. I need some time, Jazz." Amber felt tears sting her eyes. "You don't know how hard it is for me to trust. Everyone I've ever trusted has betrayed me."

"I didn't betray you." Desmon's voice was still inhuman, low with insult.

"I know." Amber turned back to him, and tears rolled down her cheeks against her will as she looked up at him. His face was mostly human now, but his eyes were still wolf-like. "I do know, Desmon. I understand you were protecting me. I shouldn't have left, but I did, and I let my ex-husband hurt me and destroy my self-esteem in the process. You have no idea how cruel he was."

Desmon growled, showing off long teeth.

"I could be wrong, but I don't think this is helping his problem," Jazz said dryly. "He's not your ex-husband. Desmon has integrity. He would never hurt you. Male wolves go insane when they're separated from their mates. As you can see, his need for you is unbending, even after all these years. He's not human. Not even a little."

Amber turned back to Jazz and reminded him, "His mother was human."

"His mother was a *wolf* when she had him. Nesso turned her right away when they mated. Desmon's not just a werewolf, he's not even an ordinary alpha werewolf. He's the strongest alpha I know, and I'm telling you that he's a danger as long as he knows his very vulnerable human mate is unclaimed and unprotected."

Amber nodded, knowing he was telling the truth.

Desmon had just tried to kill his best friend because of her.

"Can I have a week?" she asked hopefully, part of her still clinging to the dreams of her youth. "My people don't have instincts like wolves do. We need dates and flowers and long nights snuggled under the covers watching movies together, so we know we're making the right choice."

"The right choice...like you made with your ex-husband?" Jazz asked darkly.

"Shut up, Jazz," Desmon growled at his friend. "My father used to buy my mother flowers and go on dates with her. If he could play human for her, I can do the same for Amber."

Jazz sighed as he looked at the two of them. Then he wiped at the blood running down his arm again.

"I'm sorry. It's a bad time of the month," Jazz mumbled as he stared at the sticky crimson stain on his open palm. "The fight wasn't all your fault. I egged you on."

"Bad time of the month?" Amber questioned. "Is there wolf PMS I need to know about?"

"Sort of," Desmon explained behind her in that growly alpha-wolf voice. "It's a full moon tonight. We're susceptible to it. It forces our inner wolves closer to the surface. Makes us more carnal."

"I guess that part of the legend is true," Amber whispered. "How strange."

"Not really. Humans are susceptible to the full moon, too. We're just more in tune with our animal instincts." Jazz looked at his bloody arm again, sadness suddenly written all over his face. "I'm feeling confrontational, too. It's hard for me to understand why you won't claim your mate if you have her in front of you. On a full moon, my wolf gets bitter."

"That's understandable." Desmon sighed. "You should go to Mike and get that stitched up so it won't scar before it heals."

Jazz shrugged, like he could care less about a scar, but he got to his feet anyway. He walked to the entryway, but looked back at them when he reached the front door. "I'm right about this. You two need to either mate or separate." Jazz gave Amber a sympathetic look. "Desmon's wolf has been without his mate for too long."

"I just need a week," Amber promised, hoping it would be enough. "That's all I'm asking for."

Jazz nodded in understanding before he turned the knob and left without arguing.

8

*D*esmon and Amber stood there in silence afterward. She was trying to deal with the turbulent wash of emotions that were probably clouding her good judgment. Desmon was obviously having the same problem.

He left to go to the bathroom and wash up.

Desmon finally broke the silence when he came back. "I'm sorry."

"I am too." She turned back to him, seeing nothing but a watery blur when tears threatened without warning. "You should've picked one of your own kind instead of me. Everything that's happened to us is because I'm human. I bet you wish I didn't find you injured that day."

"Hey." Desmon stepped forward and wrapped his big strong arms around her. "I've never once wished that. Not once, Ams. Most days, you were the only thing I had to look forward to when I was a pup. When my dad was killed, you were the one who held me and let me be weak. Who knows what I would've turned into if I didn't have your humanity to soothe me as a child?"

Amber remembered the day Desmon came to her, sitting in their secret hideout, sobbing on her shoulder after his father was killed. At ten, she hadn't known how to soothe a loss that horrific, but she'd stroked his hair and let him cry until he'd finally fallen asleep curled on his side, with his head resting on her leg.

"Mourning your father is not a weakness, Des," she reminded him softly, her heart hurting at the memory. "I would've been worried about you if you didn't cry."

"At that time, in this pack, it *was* a weakness. You don't know what we dealt with after Albert took over. I never told you because it was too horrific." Desmon squeezed her tighter, but he looked away like he couldn't bare for her to see him when he confessed, "He took my mother after he claimed the pack. He attempted to force a mating, but her wolf would never accept him, no matter how hard he tried."

"Did he rape her?" Amber asked in shock.

"He fed her his blood. She was in bloodlust, but she was also in mourning over my father. Then, when she got pregnant, he was hopeful that at least he would have another son, but Hope was born instead."

Amber stared at him in disbelief. "You have a sister?"

Desmon nodded. "Yes, I do."

"Oh my God. She's Jazz's sister, too." Amber was surprised he hadn't mentioned his sister before now. "Why didn't I see her at the funeral?"

"Albert was so disgusted with my mother for having a girl and constantly denying his mating attempts, even in throes of bloodlust, that he gave up and publicly rejected her. After that, you honestly wouldn't believe how low her pack status was."

"How low was it?" Amber asked, eyes wide.

"He marked her as a pack whore." Desmon looked away, the pain showing on his face. "That's how he controlled me afterward. As long as I went along with his will, he wouldn't let his enforcer's use her. If I behaved, they left my mother alone. She and my sister were safe, but only if I was loyal. I risked *everything* when I went after Albert. I was so young, so fucking angry. I didn't think it through like I should've, but I got lucky. What would've happened to my mother and Hope if we hadn't won? I can't even think about it."

"My God, Des." Amber's heart hurt for him. So young, and forced to protect his mother from something unimaginable. "I'm so sorry."

"After I killed Albert, Jazz and I took the pack. We sent my mother and Hope away. We had to. They were in danger here, especially marked like my mother was." Desmon shrugged, like he'd long ago accepted the pain. "And my mom had spent most of her time locked up without freedom under that asshole's rule. She and my sister deserved real lives.

"We were fortunate to find a modern pack in Arizona, far enough away to keep them safe from wolves hungry for a territory war. More importantly, the Hunter pack doesn't allow their males to fuck a woman just because of a mark on her body. They've taken in a lot of marked refugees. It won them sanctuary pack status, which earns the Hunter pack extra protection from the alpha council. It's a safe place to be, and my mom and Hope like it there. I visit them, and so does Jazz. Their alpha lost his mate a few years ago, and he and my mother are close."

"They're mated?"

"It's very difficult for a wolf to get over the loss of a mate. Usually, it's only having young pups, like my mother did, that keeps them alive. And if they do survive, it's almost impossible for them to mate a second time. But they comfort each other."

"They're lovers," Amber clarified.

Desmon nodded again. "She lives with him, and he's a good wolf. He protects Hope like a daughter, which is not easy these days. She's more than old enough to attract male attention. I won't lie to you, Amber, pack life isn't easy on females."

"Your pack's not the same as Albert's." Amber knew it was true. "You protect the women. You've even been protecting my sisters, and you had no responsibility to them. You tried to make sure Merl didn't hurt Katie, even if she was making a massively bad life choice by dating that jerk."

"I try." Desmon sighed. "I don't always succeed, but I do my best. I promise to do everything in my power to keep you safe and happy."

"I want to believe that." Tears rolled down her cheeks. "Jeff

LAURANN DOHNER & KELE MOON

promised me that once, too, Des. I need to re-learn how to trust, but I'm trying."

"I know." Desmon brushed the hair off her neck, his fingers trailing down her throat, leaving a tingle of pleasure in their wake. "You need a week." Desmon's voice was a little growly, but he surprised her by saying, "That's more than fair." He pulled the edge of her dress aside, exposing her shoulder, and then kissing it. "Is fucking included in your week?"

She snorted in amusement. "Only if you play your cards right."

Desmon slid one rough hand up her thigh and nipped at the curve of her neck. Her breath caught as a rush of lust flooded her senses. It should have been impossible, considering the force of her last orgasm, but she was already wet and aching with very little effort on Desmon's part.

"Smells like I'm playing my cards right." Desmon brushed his fingers against the soft cotton between her thighs. "Feels like it, too."

She should be embarrassed, because she was so very wet, but she wasn't. Instead, she had to ask, "Did biting me cause bloodlust again?"

"No, this is just chemistry." Desmon nipped at her neck again, his breath warm against her ear. "This is what happens when real mates connect. This'll never fade away, as it does for most humans. I'll never stop needing you." He pushed his hips against the small of her back, letting her feel the hard outline of his cock through his suit. "You're all I've ever wanted."

God, she hoped he was telling the truth, because she felt all her carefully erected walls falling for Desmon. Too much, too soon, but she couldn't seem to stop it from happening. She wasn't even sure she *wanted* to stop it. Not when she felt as alive as she did. The lust was thick in the air around them, so real Amber felt like she could almost touch it.

The fight with Jazz must've left Desmon more primal than he'd been that first night when the bloodlust forced them together. While still kissing her neck, he slipped one hand under her dress. Then he started tugging on her panties impatiently, pulling them down her thighs. He fisted her hair with his other hand, not hard, but firm enough to force her head back, and damned if she didn't let him.

"Tell me to stop if it gets too rough." His voice was a low growl of desire, more wolf than man, but his words sounded like a plea rather than an offer. "I'd never force you. *Never*. My wolf hears you. Both sides of me respond, I promise."

She remembered what he told her about his mother and Albert. She wanted to somehow communicate that it was okay. If she was considering tying herself to an alpha werewolf, she needed to know what it was like to have sex with one when he was more wolf than man. Still supercharged from the fight with Jazz on the day of the full moon, when he was more susceptible to the beast.

She wanted to see him at his rawest now, rather than find out later she couldn't handle it.

So, she reached back and wrapped an arm around Desmon. He leaned into her with a groan, his cock still hard and thick against the small of her back, beneath his suit pants.

She summed up all her reassurance by whispering breathlessly, "You're wearing too many clothes, Des."

He must've understood that it was okay, because his hold on her hair got a little tighter, a little more forceful, as he started kissing and nipping at her neck once more. She let herself feel it rather than think, making herself wholly present with the werewolf she suspected she may still love—even after all these years.

He broke the skin only once, his teething sinking into the tender flesh at the other side of her neck, like a part of him wanted to leave his mark in both places. The bite wasn't as deep, but the pleasure rush was still unmistakable, and she cried out from it.

He stepped back too soon, leaving her feeling empty.

She turned around at the sound of ripping fabric and watched Desmon pull at his white button-down shirt. His jacket was already on the ground. His eyes were wild and wolf-like, making him look savage. He seemed to flash as she stared at him, the bones in his face changing slightly, and she realized a part of him wanted to shift.

"Don't look at me." Desmon used his wolf voice as he grabbed her and turned her around, holding her from behind.

Then he was pulling at her dress, the delicate fabric tearing under his alpha-wolf strength. Her bra was tossed aside next, but she still had her sandals on when Desmon pulled her down with him and the two of them fell to their knees.

He never bothered ridding himself of his pants. There was suddenly no time, just the sound of a zipper being lowered. She heard the rip of a condom being opened, then Desmon was there. Over her. His scent surrounding her. His grip on her hip was harsh. His hold on her hair was unforgiving, but she still moaned from the pure, unfettered pleasure that washed over her when he pushed in.

She was so wet. He was so hard, and the feel of his thick head pushing in was almost too much. She shuddered, pushing back against him, silently begging for more. Desmon gave in to his wolf and took her completely, this time like a beast, instead of the man who'd made love to her the last time.

He was fucking her, forcing the sharp gasps of ecstasy out of her with every harsh slap of his hips against hers. His low, masculine, growls only fueled the fire, and it spiraled quickly, consuming both of them. Amber was half out of her mind with the need to come, her entire body tight, shaking.

From far away, she heard the soft, breathless begging, and realized the voice was hers.

Please.

God, Des.

Right there.

She gasped and reached back, digging her nails into his thigh, breaking skin when he hit the same spot over and over again, stealing her breath. She didn't care, because the bliss was like the throb of her heartbeat, harder, louder, faster, until it was suddenly everywhere

She cried out when she shattered.

And dragged Desmon down with her.

His body tensed. He thrust his hips harder, faster against hers, using his hold on her hair to force her head back. Desmon growled, sounding completely inhuman. His breath was warm against the curve of her neck. She could practically feel his teeth against her tender skin, but he turned his face at the last minute and they rode out the storm like that.

When the pleasure started to fan out, settling down the soft flickers of contentment, Amber felt Desmon's cheek against the back of her shoulder. The brush of stubble that felt more human than werewolf. Even now, she knew he was fighting his urges—for her.

"You didn't bite me," she whispered, knowing she was saying it more for herself than him.

"No, I didn't." There was still the growl of wolf in his voice. "I promised." He caressed her hair, brushing it off her sweaty forehead. "And I keep my promises."

God, Amber could feel herself falling for this werewolf.

Too fast.

Warning bells were going off everywhere, but all she did was sigh. "I know, Des."

~

Hot and cold, the wolf under Desmon's skin was slowly going insane.

So fucking pleased to have Amber curled up next to him, her skin still flushed pink from climaxing after Desmon took her to bed and made love to her like a human. And so goddamn miserable, because she still wasn't his—even after he'd fucked her like a wolf on the floor in the living room.

He trailed his fingers over the curve of her neck, admiring the tiny marks left from tasting her, and the wolf nearly howled.

Mine.

It was a chant in his head that started the moment he saw her in the bar, and it got louder every passing second that he didn't claim her.

"You okay?" Amber's voice was soft, sleepy with the sated hum of too much sex.

"I'm great. Why?"

"You made a sound."

"A sound?" he mumbled, and traced the mark on her neck again, not really listening.

Mine!

"Like a growl." Amber looked at him over her bare shoulder, gray eyes heavy lidded, blonde hair tousled as she studied him. "What are you thinking about?"

"Nothing." Desmon dropped his hand, realizing he'd been admiring the bite mark, something a human might find a little scary. "Just—looking at you."

Amber arched an eyebrow at him. "You're thinking wolf thoughts, aren't you?"

"I'm always thinking wolf thoughts." He gave her a pointed look, even if he knew he was likely hurting his case. "I'm a wolf."

Amber turned back around, and he wasn't sure if she was hiding from the truth or accepting it. Then she brushed her hair off her neck, exposing the bite mark again, like she knew all along what he was looking at.

Desmon went back to caressing her neck longingly.

It will only be a week.

The wolf under his skin howled.

MINE!

"You made the sound again."

"Yeah," he grunted, because he wasn't sure there was anything to be done for it. "Let's talk about our week. Can I take you out tomorrow night? Maybe to Vigo's Steakhouse."

"Fancy." A smile sounded in Amber's voice. "But I don't think a fifty-dollar steak is necessary. I'd say that was excessive."

He frowned at her, realizing she was serious.

"Hey." Desmon caught her shoulder, forcing Amber to roll over and look at him. "You don't think *a steak* is necessary? What exactly did you mean, then, when you asked to be courted like a human?"

"I wasn't talking about you losing a bunch of money." She laughed. "We can just spend time together. No sense wasting it on some place like Vigo's."

"Amber, I would give up everything I own tomorrow if I thought it would convince you to be mine. Literally, I'd do it without thinking. I can make more money—I can't get another mate. What do you think I've been telling you? I had already planned on dying lonely until you showed up. My wolf decided a long time ago who his mate is, and you think a steak is too much?"

Amber rolled back over, and her voice cracked with emotion as she whispered, "Your wolf has bad taste, then."

"No, he doesn't." Desmon kissed her neck and ran a hand over her bare hip beneath the blanket as his cock stirred again. "You're worth a steak, Ams. You're worth the whole fucking restaurant, and I want to kill your ex-husband for making you question that."

"You sound serious."

"Trust me, if you knew how serious..." The growl was back in his voice. "It's only because he has young that I'm asking you to make sure your ex-husband and I never end up in the same room together."

"He doesn't take care of his young." Amber laughed bitterly. "He sends her a court-ordered check for that little boy, and that's it."

"I don't understand human men," Desmon admitted with a frown. "I thought it was a nature thing, but I guess humans are different than the rest of us if they don't want young. Look at all the hell Albert put my family through for a son. Even the worst of our kind still want pups—especially male pups."

Amber looked at him again over her shoulder. "Do you want male pups?"

"I can't lie to you and say I don't." He caressed her hair again, tucking a strand behind her ear. "I'm not Albert. They wouldn't have to be males. Any pup would be an incredible gift. I would love to have a daughter with you, even if she'd be more difficult to protect. It would be an honor. What about you? Is that something you think about?"

"I wanted children." Her voice was soft. "Jeff didn't, and I respected his wishes. I was glad later. It made it easier for the divorce, but I know I'm getting older."

"You could have them for a long time if you mated me." Desmon grinned at her. "Mary just gave her mate, Douglas, another daughter last night. Mary's ninety-five, and that's still young for a bitch."

Amber smiled back at him. "That's a compelling argument, even if you did just call her a bitch."

"Bitch isn't an insult in our world. You'd have time, that's all I'm saying." He shrugged. "You wouldn't be tied to that human biological clock."

"I'll let you buy me a steak." Amber's smile grew wider. "We could even do it tonight if you wanted."

"I wish, Angel." Desmon winced. "I have pack obligations tonight."

"The full moon." Amber nodded. "I remember."

"Yeah." He ran a hand down her bare arm, admiring her soft skin. "And after tonight, I'm all yours."

"Scared to be with me on the full moon?" she asked curiously.

"That too." He flinched again, because it wasn't a lie. "I do actually have to be on alpha duty tonight. Weres are well known for finding trouble during full moon—and they're capable of getting in plenty of difficult situations without it. You honestly wouldn't believe some of the shit that happens."

Amber snuggled into him and pulled the sheet back over both of them. When Desmon dropped his head down on the pillow next to her and pulled Amber's naked body more tightly against his, she said sleepily, "Sounds like you already have pups, a whole pack of them."

He snorted. "If you only knew how true that is."

9

"I know everyone says a Liberal Arts degree is useless." Bea sat on a bench in the clothing store and leaned over to look in the mirror next to her in a way that was very typical for a seventeen-year-old girl. She tucked strands of her long, curly blonde hair behind her ears, and then studied her teeth. "The truth is, if money didn't matter, I would love to be an English major. Crazy, right?"

"Not that crazy. And who's everyone?" Amber pulled a dress off the rack and held it out. The red was bolder than she usually would've picked, but for some reason, she liked it, and it was in her size. "There are plenty of successful people with Liberal Arts degrees. If you want to major in English, then that's what you should do, Bea."

"God, I hope I get this foundation scholarship." Bea closed her eyes and leaned back against the wall. "I know it's just community college, but every little bit helps."

"I already told you I would help with college." Amber held the dress up to herself. "I'd pay for Katie, too, if she would consider going."

"She won't. Katie had a really hard time in high school. She would never want to take classes over at Conley." Bea tilted her head and looked at the dress in Amber's hand. "You should try it on."

It wasn't just brighter than she was used to wearing, it was also considerably tighter and shorter. She would've never gone out with Jeff in it, but the thought of wearing it for Desmon stole her breath. She kept remembering the way he watched her on the porch earlier, pupils dilated, feral and hungry, before he'd warned her that wolves could smell desire.

"Desmon will like it," Bea added, as though reading her mind.

"That's not the reason I'd buy it." Amber gave her sister a firm look, but then completely ruined the lie. "I will try it on, but it's just to see. It's not about him, it's about me."

Bea bit her lip to hide her smile. "Okay."

Amber was quick about trying on the dress. Once she had it on, the tight red material left her feeling exposed, but that's what made it thrilling. She stood on her toes and turned sideways to see what she would look like in heels wearing this dress to Vigo's Steakhouse.

It was certainly bold, but it was her first official date with Desmon.

She felt the warm tingle of lust wash over her when she imagined Desmon pulling the thin spaghetti straps down and kissing her shoulder. Amber touched the spot where he'd bitten her earlier and felt none of the tenderness. She looked in the mirror and discovered the mark was barely there now, when it had been a noticeable bruise before she'd left the house. He did something to heal her, which wasn't nearly as unnerving as it should've been.

"Let's see it," Bea called out.

Amber opened the dressing room door. She stood on her toes, so her sister could get the full effect. Her legs weren't as long as she'd like for this particular dress, but with the right heels, it could work.

Bea grinned. "That's a dress to make a guy fall in love with you."

Amber just sighed rather than respond. She couldn't really argue when she was out shopping for a dress specifically for a date with Desmon. To hide her blush, she glanced around the shop, noticing a man standing next to the rack she'd gotten the dress from. He was tall, dressed simply in a red t-shirt and jeans, and the way he sniffed at the rack would've been bizarre if Amber didn't know werewolves ran wild everywhere around here.

"Come help me unzip it." Amber grabbed Bea's hand and dragged her back into the dressing room.

Bea obviously saw the strange werewolf and understood. She didn't argue or fight Amber's pull. When the two of them were alone in the tiny dressing room, Amber whispered to her sister, "Do you know him?"

Bea shook her head and put her finger to her lips. Then she spoke casually, but pointed to the direction of the stranger. "The earphones work really well. They let you *hear everything*."

Amber knew Bea was trying to warn her that the werewolves could hear well, so she nodded in silent understanding and turned around, letting Bea help with the zipper since she was there. Amber was quick about putting her clothes on, hoping to God that strange guy was gone when they got out.

"It's okay," Bea assured her, like this wasn't the first run-in she'd had. "These things happen to Katie, too. They can tell who you spend time with."

The man wasn't there when they walked out of the dressing room, and Amber breathed a sigh of relief. Needing a distraction, she decided, "I think I'm going to buy the dress."

"You *need* that dress," Bea agreed. "Desmon's going to lose his mind when he sees you in it."

"Well, don't say that. We all want Desmon to stay sane." Amber shuddered, thinking of Desmon's fight with Jazz earlier. "Trust me, you don't want to see the alternative."

"What happened?" Bea seemed curious

"Nothing major, but it did remind me who I was dealing with."

Amber searched for her credit card. The woman behind the counter smiled, rang her up, and put the dress in a bag. With Bea at her side, they left the shop.

She was closing her purse when Bea grabbed her arm as they reached the sidewalk. Amber glanced up and gasped as the man from the dress shop was suddenly right there, stepping between her and Bea like it was his place.

He sniffed at Amber's neck.

"Excuse you." She pushed him away. "You're in my personal space, buddy."

"Yeah, you're being really obvious." Bea added in a whisper, "And we're protected. Desmon Nightwind's a *very* good friend."

"Not *that* good. She's not very protected right now," he hissed back. Then he sniffed at Amber again before tilting his head, studying her. "Bored with you already? You're not bad for a human."

Amber didn't want to upset the stranger, because she'd seen first-hand how mindless werewolves could get when truly angry.

She glanced around the street they stood next to, and then looked at the werewolf in warning, trying to convey that she would scream out if he did anything stupid. He was a big guy, easily as tall as Desmon, just not nearly as broad shouldered. He had short brown hair that was neatly styled, and the brush of a five o'clock shadow on his chin, but he wasn't any hairier than that. It should've been reassuring, but his pupils were dilated like Desmon's got when he was feeling more wolf-like.

Amber tugged on Bea's arm, making her younger sister stand behind her, away from the stranger.

"My name's Gary, and *I'm* your friend." Gary's eyes seemed to normalize, as though he knew seeing his wild side had scared Amber. "Desmon Nightwind's the one who's not your friend. They kill human females, you know. Even the ones they call pack. Not the best pack to bed hop in." He raised his eyebrows in warning. "It's true, ask anyone. They killed that human girl who lived with them some years back. That's a big risk for a cute little thing like you."

Amber snapped, "Desmon would never do that."

"Sure he would, because guess what, princess? Desmon Nightwind is a dick." Gary laughed, before he suddenly sobered. "My sister would've made a strong mate to him. Bonding with her would've brought peace to this entire area, but he rejected her *after* he screwed her. He humiliated her, just like he's humiliating *you*."

Amber felt her cheeks burn for a different reason when she realized this werewolf was smelling Desmon on her. Nothing was private with these wolves.

Bea leaned past Amber and glared at the werewolf. "We're protected by the Nightwinds, and that's exactly how we like it."

"It doesn't smell like she's protected." The werewolf's voice was a low growl. "I bet you don't even have a wolf to spend the full moon with, do you? The most romantic night of the month." Something must've showed on Amber's face, because Gary snorted in knowing. "I told you they're not worth your loyalty."

"He has responsibilities." Amber stood tall, keeping her shoulders back even though she remembered making the same type of excuses for her ex-husband.

"I dare you to follow Desmon to the edge of Hader Ravine tonight, on the north end, just past Mike's Quick Mart. Follow the fence behind the gas station about a half mile. There's a spot at the edge of the woods where they use the clearing to start the run. Wait until the full moon is cresting, and see how loyal he is to you."

"He's lying." Bea gave Amber a look of warning. "Mike's Quick Mart is the marker for the woods between Nightwind and Goodwin territory. Desmon wouldn't be stupid enough to start the run there."

"You'd think not, but he does. Every single month." Gary didn't look too bothered by it as he directed his attention back to Amber. "They don't want you out there, 'cause they only fuck bitches for the full moon—and they don't change their human whores. They keep you weak and leave you home for the party. Go see what I'm talking about tonight, human, then decide who you trust."

"Okay, maybe we will," Amber lied, as she grabbed Bea's arm. She kept walking, wanting to get away from him to reach her car. "Nice talking to you."

Bea followed Amber across the street before Bea asked, "Is he gone?"

Amber finally dared to glance back. "I don't see him."

"I know he's one of the Goodwins." Bea stopped in front of a bakery shop and looked around quickly before she went on. "There's a really dangerous territory standoff happening with them right now, Amber. Desmon is going to freak when he finds out we came into town alone after we promised we'd stay on pack land. Katie says alpha wolves aren't used to their orders not being followed. It doesn't matter if we're pack or not, it's safer to do what he says."

Amber threw up her hands. "I don't want to hear about Desmon needing to be obeyed."

"It's part of their pack mentality. That's how it all works. The wolves in his pack obey him. It's nature. Katie says to always follow orders when Desmon gives them, so we don't stand out as different."

"What?" Amber stopped next to her car and gripped her sister's arm. "She told you to follow Desmon's orders, no matter what? This man she barely knows? She thinks you should just do whatever he tells you to, so you don't stand out as different?"

Bea nodded. "Because we can't afford to lose pack protection."

"I don't know where Katie got such awful, unhealthy ideas, but it's probably part of the reason she was with Merl. Bea, you do not have to follow Desmon's orders—or anyone else's, for that matter. Never do *anything* you're not comfortable with."

"She didn't mean it like that." Bea rolled her eyes. "It's Desmon. She knew he wouldn't try to take advantage of me like that."

"I know." Amber sighed, because she did know it. "Thank God Desmon's the one in charge. She could've sworn both your loyalties to someone like Merl. Katie's survival instincts suck. Let's take off, unless you need anything."

"Let's just go," Bea agreed quickly. "Are you going to tell Desmon?"

"No, I'm not going to call him and have to apologize for not obeying him. I'm trying to *like* Desmon this week." Amber gave her sister a smile and admitted. "I kind of want to give him a fighting chance for this whole mate thing."

"That'd be awesome." Bea grinned too. "Then you'd have to stay."

"Desmon or no Desmon, you won't lose me that easily." Amber

wrapped an arm around her sister, pulling her close once more. Despite the run-in, she was in an incredibly upbeat mood, and she didn't want werewolf drama to ruin it. "Let's get back to the house before he knows we left. What happened today...we'll just keep Gary to ourselves."

Bea nodded. "Works for me."

10
---

*D*esmon skipped the pack house and showered at home after he left Amber's. He didn't want to deal with all the single men in the pack house teasing him over how strongly he smelled of sex—like they had the first time he and Amber had gotten together. Usually, it wouldn't bother him, but right now, he didn't trust himself after attacking his best friend. Jazz was right, on the day of the full moon, with an unclaimed human mate, Desmon was dangerous.

He didn't spend much time in the two-story house his father built with the help of his pack. Even if it was beautiful, everything about the house hurt him. He had been happy there as a pup, but Albert destroyed everything the day he and his group of new enforcers killed their alpha, five on one.

Since his mother and sister left, Desmon rarely slept there. Even more so than usual, Desmon couldn't get out of the house fast enough. He was running from a lot of things, but fortunately, the work of an alpha was never done.

He threw himself into solving problems for the rest of the afternoon, and even went so far as to meet with the accountant, something he had been putting off for a week. That ended up being a bad idea. Their pack accountant was a wolf, so he understood it was a bad time of the month, but Desmon's growling, short temper still wasn't a good mix for discussing their rising property taxes.

Desmon looked out his window, watching Harvey get into his car. He was still so abnormally frustrated, and angry at Harvey, even though it wasn't his fault the property taxes in California were insane.

Desmon had to give up on work, at least for a little while. "I'm going for a run."

"Okay, Alpha," Janie, his secretary, called back. "Should I send all the phone messages to Alpha Jazz?"

Desmon winced, remembering the fight earlier. "No, just the important ones."

The constant smack of Janie's gum stopped, and Desmon came to his office door to see her sitting at the front desk looking at him with concern. "How will I know which ones are the important ones?"

Desmon arched an eyebrow at her. "How do you usually tell if it's something I need to pay attention to? Like a war declaration from the Goodwins, or a California tax lien on the pack houses?"

Janie stared at him, green eyes wide, pupils dilated as she popped her gum again, letting her wolf show while she thought over his words. Janie was only nineteen. She hadn't learned to disguise herself as well as some of the other young wolves in the pack, so Desmon kept her close, more so because she lost her father as a pup. Janie was one of the few unmated females in the pack. She also had a damsel-in-distress, omega-wolf-in-need-of-a-protector vibe that male weres went nuts for, particularly beta wolves. Alpha males tended to go for females with stronger personalities. Stubborn, determined, spines of steel, could manage a pack if needed...independent.

Desmon equally loved and hated Amber's independence.

"Oh!" Janie pointed at Desmon. "If it's something that'll make you growl. Like, if the Alpha Council calls, and I'll think, 'He's going to be growly about this. Time for a lunch break.' Stuff like that, right?"

"I'm not growly, but yes, the Alpha Council would be one to text Jazz about. If it's really important, he'll be able to find me. Don't forget—"

"A human named Amber, I know. Tell you immediately if she calls." Janie rolled her eyes. "So, if she's human, she's not going to the running?"

"Nope." Desmon shrugged, because he *was* disappointed about it.

"Bummer."

Janie looked to her phone. The younger weres were much better about technology than the older ones. Desmon just wasn't sure if that was a good or bad thing.

Then, she added, "I was thinking of running near the border tonight."

Desmon growled.

She smiled and pointed, looking pleased that her running activities was something important enough to growl about.

"You've had at least twenty running offers, and those are just the ones I've heard of." Desmon rubbed his forehead. "Janie, I'd really like you staying inland, with a wolf you know will be kind. There're a lot of betas who would take advantage of a young omega on the full moon."

"I'm not stupid, Alpha. I know it's a risk, but my mate's not in Nightwind. I'd feel something when he walked into the room, right?" Janie looked up at Desmon. "I'd know if he was mine, wouldn't I?"

Desmon stood there, thinking of the feeling he got when he was near Amber. He nodded, because he couldn't lie to her about it. "Yes, you'd know something. It's very noticeable."

"Even without mating with him?" Janie pressed, green eyes wide, pupils dilated once more as the wolf in her lit up at the idea of finding a mate. "I'd still feel it, just being next to him?"

"You'd feel it," Desmon had to reluctantly admit, even if it made his life more difficult. "You'd *want* to make a running date with him."

"There's no one in this pack I want to make a date with. And those offers you heard, they know I'm not theirs, either. They want to do it because their friends told them omegas are submissive and do whatever they want on the running. I'm not into that, not without a bond. I'd rather go near the border. Maybe I'll get lucky and find the one."

"Landing in Goodwin because of a mating would not be lucky. You're too young to remember what it was like before Albert—"

"I remember," Janie whispered.

Desmon winced, because Albert made her father an enforcer on the north end, knowing he was an omega wolf. Lyle didn't last three years, which was a lot longer than Albert had anticipated. That was the most dangerous assignment in their pack. It had been a death sentence for a wolf who wasn't naturally a fighter, but like Janie, her father Lyle had also been surprisingly tenacious.

"Goodwins are like Albert. Their ideas are very backwards," Desmon warned her. "We do the runnings on the border to give the Goodwin females a chance to get out, not to send ours to Goodwin. Being an omega wolf in Goodwin would be terrible, even if you had a mate. I would be doing your father a huge disservice to let you look for your mate over there."

She tilted her head, as though considering it, and then suggested, "I could go into town."

Desmon had a feeling he'd played right into her hands, and he growled again.

"Sara and Dawn both have motel rooms across the street from Pacers, and I love that human club. The music's so much better than at The Barn, and it's mostly human men, and they're closer to my age. If I find one I like, I won't bite, even if he smells really yummy, and—"

Desmon held up his hands. "Let me think about it, Janie."

"Jason has a human mate," Janie went on, as if she hadn't heard him. "And now *your* mate is human, and—"

"I'm extra frustrated today." Desmon gave her a look. "And very aware that allowing a nineteen-year-old wolf to run wild around town looking for an unsuspecting human male to keep her company for the full moon is a massive mistake waiting to happen. I'd need to be half delirious with exhaustion to consider saying yes to that."

"Go run." Janie gestured to the door without hesitation, clearly hoping he would manage to run until he was delirious. "I'll text Jazz with the important stuff."

He didn't need to hear the suggestion twice, and left his cell phone on her desk for safekeeping.

Desmon's office was located in the center of pack land, but he still encouraged his wolves to be cautious about shifting out in the open.

Most of them weren't.

Around the corner, away from Janie's window, there was a walled-off area, just in case unsuspecting humans wandered in. It looked like a small outside dressing room. It had a bench and a coat rack, because there were lots of times Desmon needed to take off in fur to deal with an issue.

Once he was naked, he didn't waste time, and was quickly a wolf instead of a man. Then he ran hard toward the woods. Desmon took the scenic route, going full throttle the whole time. He went all the way to the north end of the border. The trees became denser. The ground was mossy, now more mud than dirt, because the branches hid most of the dying afternoon sun. It was a dark, depressing side of their territory, one most of their pack wouldn't venture out to on a dare.

The two-story cabin was hidden by a canopy of trees. The porch was swept. The leaves that had fallen on the surrounding property were raked up in a small heap off to the right side of the building. A large pile of chopped wood was stacked up next to it, and smoke from the chimney betrayed how well used that firewood actually was.

Jason and Brandie were the closest neighbors, but their land had plenty of sunlight.

Desmon smelled venison cooking and realized he was famished. For some reason, when the wolf was at the forefront of his mind, he was always on the lookout for food. It likely had to do with survival. Alphas were as simple as any other wolf. Their priorities could be narrowed down to three things—eat, fuck, protect the pack, not always in that order. When he was feeling vulnerable, his animal half was doubly determined to keep his body powerful and resilient.

He didn't have to change forms to knock. The door opened and Miles stood there, bare-chested and barefoot, in only his jeans. He didn't hide the scars on his shoulders, chest and stomach that kept him from shifting. His long dark hair, nearly identical to Desmon's, was tied back, leaving his marred face more visible.

Usually, Miles didn't open the door so easily, but Desmon was his cousin and, more importantly, the two of them were friends from puppyhood. Desmon didn't have to beg to be let in like others.

"Surprised to see you in the north end. Thought you'd be busy with other things after hearing the shit going around about you." Miles's voice was the low growl of a lone wolf, more feral than others in the pack. "Hungry?"

Desmon shifted and stood to his full human height. "Starving."

"I figured." Miles opened his door wider, inviting Desmon in. He pointed toward his bedroom. "I have jeans in my bottom drawer."

Desmon didn't ask where Miles had heard about his issues, though it was odd for the gossip to reach him clear out in the north end. Miles didn't talk to anyone.

After Desmon pulled on some jeans, he walked into the kitchen. Miles had divided the venison onto two plates and set the table.

"There's coffee in the pot, go ahead and grab some." Miles pointed to a coffeepot in the corner. "Smells like you didn't get much sleep last night."

Desmon poured himself a cup of coffee, black, and sat across from Miles.

"I actually slept fine last night. What you smell happened this afternoon, and I did take a shower before I came over here." Desmon took a bite, impressed. "This is really good."

"Thanks. Your shower didn't work, by the way. I can still scent your human on you."

"I've been at work all day but no one said anything. Only you can smell her." Desmon couldn't hide his admiration. "You're the best scenter in California."

Miles took a bite. "Gary Goodwin's better than me."

Desmon flinched, because Miles wasn't wrong. All the Goodwins were amazing scenters, but Gary Goodwin was in a class by himself.

"I hate Gary Goodwin. I hate him more than Leroy. Arrogant bastard. It irritates the fuck out of me that he's as good as he is."

Desmon's voice was low, slightly inhuman with irritation. "Why won't you teach a scenting class to the pups?"

"Do you really want me around the pups?" Miles asked darkly. "So they can run home and tell their mommies when I growl at them?"

"I'm talking about teenage pups, asshole, not toddlers."

Miles let out a low, displeased growl. "Same difference."

Desmon growled back. "You're the only one we have who could give Gary Goodwin a run for his money. It's your job as a member of this pack to help educate our young and make us stronger."

The scenting problem wasn't new, but since Amber showed up, Desmon had started getting anxious to strengthen the pack. The Nightwinds were already strong, but so were the Goodwins, and peace between the two packs was likely impossible.

Desmon wanted his pack to be the best in the area.

Invincible.

"You're teaching a scenting class, Miles." Desmon growled once more at his cousin. He knew why Miles hid out here in the north border, but it had been years since the accident. "You can suck it up and come into town twice a week and teach the older pups tracking. Your father would want you to preserve the old ways."

Miles snorted and flipped him off. "Jazz texted all your enforcers to let us know you might be aggressive for the next few days. He didn't say anything about you being psychotic."

Rather than take the high road, Desmon doubled down on his bad mood. "Jazz texted you my problems?"

"No details. Just watch your asses, don't mouth off to Des this week." Miles took a sip of his coffee. "After that, I called Jason to find out what was going on. He gave me the details on the Amber situation, which is why I'm not kicking you out of my house right now." Miles looked at Desmon sympathetically. "Am I supposed to say congratulations?"

"I guess." Desmon ran both his hands through his hair. "She's back. That's what matters. I wish I didn't have to do this running tonight. I hate leaving her."

"It's difficult to have a mate who's human." Miles pushed at his food with his fork like he was looking for something to do with his hands. "I think Jason misses the runnings, but he won't leave Brandi, and I can't blame him. I wouldn't leave my mate, either. Don't know why he won't change her."

The running was a sensitive issue with Miles, because he couldn't shift anymore, but Miles didn't let it show today. He just gave Desmon a pointed look. "If you didn't let them run so close to Goodwin territory, you wouldn't have to go babysit like you do every full moon. You could stay with your mate."

"I know, but a lot of the Goodwin females are trying to get out of that pack, and we have too many unmated males right now. They keep going into town and finding human females there, which isn't always good. Look at the whole Merl-and-Katie nightmare. She says she wants to be with him, so what can I do? I can't force her to stay away from him. It's justhuman females are so fragile."

Desmon didn't mention his own human issues with Amber, but he worried over them. It was going against everything in him to leave her alone during the running. He didn't need her to run with him, but he did want to spend the full moon doing something other than making sure young pack members didn't chase their tails into the wrong territory.

As always, Desmon thought about his mother during the years when Albert had control of her, knowing there were women in Goodwin facing the same fate. Many of them were marked as pack whores like his mother had been, and their lives were likely horrific.

"We're keeping close to the border." Desmon was talking more to himself than Miles. "Their females know where to find us if they want to try for a way out of that pack, and it is the only day of the month where our males have an excuse to be sniffing around. If a mating happens, it's not the Goodwins' place to argue with nature."

Miles rolled his eyes. "Then don't complain about babysitting."

A smartphone on the counter dinged with a message. Miles pushed away from the table and walked over to grab it. He stared at the screen with a frown and looked up at Desmon. "Jazz is asking if you're here."

Desmon sighed. "I know I need to start running with my phone."

"Buy a harness, or just borrow one of my old ones. I have extras." Miles sat back in his chair as he typed on his phone. "You could run with your phone and a gun. It'd make your life a lot easier."

Desmon let out a low, angry growl.

"You think you're too good, but I never went on an assignment without wearing one for good reason. If they're suitable enough for the enforcers of World Shifter Alliance, they're suitable enough for you, Desmon Nightwind."

"You know as well as anyone if I came at a strange shifter wearing an Alliance Enforcer harness with a weapon, I wouldn't have to fight them. They'd drop dead in terror." Desmon snorted.

"You're not wrong. No one wants to run into an Alliance Enforcer, with or without their harness. Just talking about one showing up will make a were sweat." Miles sighed nostalgically. "I miss that."

"Don't worry, you're still terrifying when you show up," Desmon snorted in amusement. "You really miss serving with them? It's such grim work."

"It's not pleasant, but it's necessary to protect our people and someone has to do it. I was planning on renewing my contract before my accident, but I know now it would have been a mistake. The ones who stay in too long, it's worse than the scars I'm stuck with. They're always primal, putting off that aggressive, territorial scent, like their pack is under attack, and not just the wolves—any shifters, even the cats.

"They lose themselves. Their only loyalty is the Alliance, and they go after every assignment like survival is at stake." Miles's phone went off again, and he picked it up to read the message. "Jazz is looking for you, speaking of the Alliance." He glanced up with a look of apprehension. "He says they called in a hazard report out here on the north end."

Desmon jumped up and went for the portable hanging by the fridge.

Before Jazz had a chance to say hello, Desmon asked, "What's the north end hazard?"

"A sleuth of were-bears who got displaced by the fires. Just figured you should know in case you stumble across them." Jazz didn't sound too concerned. "Janie says you've been gone a few hours. Are you okay?"

"I'm fine," Desmon lied, running a hand through his hair. "Tell me about the bears."

"They're following the rules, traveling in neutral territory, but they called in for permission to cross through. I gave them the go-ahead, since it was the Bear High Council asking the favor."

"I wouldn't have given them permission to cross. They could decide they like it, and then what? You think the Goodwins are bad, try being in a territory war with a group of grizzlies," Miles growled, clearly still listening in. "I'd rather fight a tiger than a grizzly."

"Bullshit." Jazz laughed. "I'd rather fight two grizzlies than a fucking tiger. I met one once, when I was helping out the Hunters in Arizona and visiting Hope. This guy was standing there, working the door at a were club in Phoenix, just chilling and watching out for humans and pups trying to get in. Nice for a cat. Seemed harmless. Then something went down, and I saw him shift. Fuck that. I'll take a bear any day. I can outrun a bear."

"Something you might not know about grizzlies." Miles actually took the phone from Desmon and spoke into the receiver, "They can run just as fast as a tiger. I've seen it with my own eyes—more than once."

"Miles, I watched that tiger jump two stories straight up without blinking, and that was *before* he'd shifted. There's not a grizzly alive who could do that." Jazz seemed bored with the conversation. "Besides, there's no grizzles stomping through your backyard. Just eight black bears and a couple of cubs. We could defend our territory if we have to, but we won't, because they're bears, and they don't bother anyone."

"Until they do."

Jazz sighed. "Man, everyone likes bears. I don't know what your problem is."

"He doesn't like *anyone*, bears included." Desmon took the phone back. "I'll run back to the office." He wanted to know if Jazz got his arm stitched, but instead asked, "Meet you there?"

"Nah, you don't have to come back. Go rest up for an hour or so before the running. Could be a long night. Janie's on the prowl to get off pack land."

"I know, and she's not wrong." Desmon closed his eyes tiredly. "Her mate's not in the pack. I have to let her out. I'd be defying nature not to."

"I'll head into town tonight and keep an eye on the females at the dance club," Jazz decided for them both. "You stick with the males at the Goodwin border, and we'll remind all the mated couples to stay inland to make our lives easier."

It was a good plan, similar to ones in the past because they had so many young wolves who were inclined to roam in new directions looking for their mates.

"I think Janie could be one female too many, because she told me Sara and Dawn have plans, too. Did you know about that?"

"No," Jazz snorted. "She forgot that part."

"That's a lot, Jazz. Plus your usual crew," Desmon said. "They'll scatter in twenty different directions, and you're susceptible, too. What if you end up distracted by a human for the night? You're not nineteen, but it happens."

"I don't screw on the full moon." An edge of darkness came into Jazz's voice when he admitted, "Wolf's too close to the surface. I won't get distracted."

Desmon understood, because his wolf was every bit as loyal as Jazz's. The only thing the full moon did was make him more despondent for his mate. If anything, being on alpha duty for the full moon was a welcome distraction. The alternative would be sitting home, horny and lonely without a mate to fuck, while stuck wholly in the mindset of the wolf, who wasn't willing to go looking for a substitute.

It really was unfair Desmon was going to miss spending their first full moon together with Amber, even if she didn't fully appreciate the significance of it.

Not that anything about the life of an alpha wolf was fair.

"Give 'em dog whistles," Miles suggested, and then took a drink of his coffee. "In case one of them loses her phone like last time."

"That's actually not a bad idea," Jazz agreed through the phone. "I'll put out check-in whistles every few hours since they can't howl in town. You can run with the harness and your cell in case I need help rounding them up, since the females are our first priority to protect."

Desmon growled.

"Just the unmated ones," Jazz clarified. "If they want to run in town, the girls can wear the whistles like necklaces, since they'll likely stay in human form."

Miles laughed. "He's growling about the harness. My father would've cut off his own tail before he wore a harness. I've never understood what the big fucking deal is. We've been settled in California for over a hundred years. The ancient ways are long gone."

"The ways aren't dead. We're both standing here, which means they're still very much alive," Desmon growled at him. "Which is why you're going to teach a scenting class to the teenage pups Monday and Friday afternoons starting this week."

"So, I'm teaching a scenting class, but you can't wear a harness to help your pack?" Miles arched an eyebrow at Desmon. "Times change, Des. Humans are closer. We have to adapt, even if that means wearing a harness. Now they're just tools, like the laptops and the phones. It's not a human leash. That symbolism is dead."

Jazz snorted in amusement. "Well, lucky for me, long-displaced Irish wolves have no ancient symbols. I have zero issues with wearing a harness if it helps me keep the horny, unmated wolves herded, and I like the idea of both of us having phones. Miles, do you have two harnesses so we can both wear one?"

"I have more than that," Miles assured him. "If Desmon can get over his shit."

"I'll wear it to carry my phone, so my mate can call me during the running," Desmon clarified with another growl, knowing he was going to have to stop at his office before the running to grab the phone he always tried so desperately to get rid of. "And that is the *only* reason I'm doing it."

"Okay, buddy." Jazz snorted with amusement. "As long as we know the reason."

11

"He's probably off fucking some Goodwin bitch at the border right this minute."

Amber stopped washing the dishes and stared at Katie, who was sitting at the kitchen counter, looking at her phone morosely. She had been waiting for a text from Merl, assuming he'd get desperate for the full moon, but thankfully, it'd been nothing but radio silence.

"You know he's," Amber paused, looking for the gentlest way possible to describe Merl, since she was trying her hardest to stay on good terms with her sister, "the worst of his kind."

Katie was quiet for a moment, before she whispered, "You say that, but you should've seen the Goodwin guys I waited on at the skin bar. Werewolves are more primal than humans, but they protect what's theirs. I was always safer with Merl. You just don't get it."

Amber did have a budding relationship with her own werewolf going, and had to point out, "I think that's total bullshit, Katie. Desmon doesn't treat me the way Merl treated you. It's not about Merl being a werewolf, it's about him being an asshole. Just because that's how your father treated our mother, doesn't mean that's how it should be."

"Great advice." Katie rolled her eyes. "Too bad we don't all have alphas banging down our doors begging to love and protect us until their dying breath. You don't even appreciate it. That's the worst part of the whole thing."

Amber turned off the faucet. "I know you felt safer being with Merl, like you needed his protection, but we're going to be okay without him. I'm glad he's staying away and maybe one day—"

"One day, what? I'll find a nice human and settle down and have a boring life," Katie barked back at her. "What if I don't want that? You expect me to go from hot were sex, to regular old human sex? Don't tell me you don't know what I'm talking about, Amber, because we all know you do."

Amber looked over her shoulder at Bea reading on the couch. She wasn't going to debate this subject in front of their youngest sister, and she wasn't even sure she was qualified. The only human she had slept with was her ex-husband, and he was pretty fucking pitiful. And the only wolf she'd slept with was Desmon, who just happened to be amazing in bed.

Not really a fair comparison between humans and werewolves.

"Maybe you'll find a nice wolf instead?" Amber lowered her voice pointedly when she turned back to Katie. "I know there are good ones in Desmon's pack. I haven't met them all, but it seems like Merl's the exception, not the rule in Nightwind. Look at Jason and Brandi. He worships her, and she's human."

Katie was quiet for a moment, before she muttered, "Maybe."

"It's true," Bea called from the chair in the living room, still holding a book, but clearly eavesdropping instead of reading. "None of the others are like Merl. Most of 'em are really nice. They like humans, especially the ones my age. I might even consider dating one, if they weren't all super shy around me."

Amber's eyes widened in concerned.

"They're not shy," Katie whispered to Amber. "Don't freak out. Desmon makes them stay away from her."

"I heard that," Bea barked, and turned around to look at them from the living room. "Is that true?"

"Teenage weres can't control their hormones like grown ones

can," Katie said impatiently. "They have to stay away, or its dangerous for them, too—Desmon's really strict with them about it. He makes damn sure none of his wolves are hurting women, especially humans. It's part of pack law. He was always after Merl over me. Bet he's glad we broke up. Probably sick of the headache."

"He's not the only one," Amber couldn't help but admit. "If you prefer wolves, you could find a better one, Katie."

"I know," Katie admitted, and raised her eyebrows. "It *is* the full moon, maybe I'll head over to the Quick Mart and see if one wanders over from the woods and finds me. All the single males run at the border now."

"I heard." Amber gave Katie a look of disbelief while her sister went back to staring at her phone, like she was waiting for it to light up with a bootie call from Merl. "Looking for fresh meat already? Or hoping to spot Merl while he's feeling frisky? Either way, you know it's a bad idea right now. You should take some time for yourself first."

"Then I need ice cream," Katie huffed in defeat. "Lots of it."

Amber went to the freezer, opening it hopefully, but found only game meat and frozen meals. She heard the jangle of keys and turned to see Katie already digging in her purse like an addict hungry for one more good ride—only she wasn't after drugs and booze like their stepfather had been.

Katie admitted Merl gave her his blood on a regular basis, and Amber could see how that could certainly become addictive.

She went to her purse hanging off the chair Katie was sitting in and shouldered it. "I'll go."

"It's raining," Katie warned her. "And you're not used to driving in the mountains anymore."

"I'll deal with it." Amber did not understand Katie's obsession with that asshole, but she did know she was going to do her best to stop Merl from hurting her sister, even if that meant going out in the rain for ice cream. "What flavor am I getting?"

"There's no bad flavor of ice cream," Katie said with a wan smile.

"Bea, any suggestions?"

"I like it all," Bea agreed with Katie. "Any ice cream is a treat."

Amber realized her sisters weren't used to indulgences, even simple ones like ice cream, and decided a trip in the rain was worth it. She didn't even bother with an umbrella, even though it was coming down hard.

By the time she got behind the wheel of her Benz, Amber was dripping wet. She sat there for a moment, staring at the house she grew up in while the storm beat against the car.

Even with all the work they'd done to it, something about the simple wooden dwelling seemed sinister. She couldn't blame herself for leaving after the hell she went through growing up, but the guilt still burned in her stomach.

Suddenly depressed and uncomfortable, Amber found herself missing Desmon. Being in his arms made her feel so safe and protected, like everything could actually be alright.

Is it love?

Maybe this is what it felt like, that warm, steady pull toward the other person that always made her feel safer and happier with him than without him. Or maybe she was nuts to trust it.

Maybe love doesn't exist.

She started the car and pulled out of the driveway, still pondering it. The road was already under water in the lower sections. Even if the state had repaved it during the time she'd been gone, they were still in a rural section of the mountains. If it kept raining like this, the flooding would start. Just what they needed.

Driving slowly, focused on the road like she was, the thump against her car made Amber gasp.

She slammed on her breaks, making the car fishtail. Her heart started pumping hard and fast against her chest as she put the car in park and threw open the driver's side door.

"Please don't be a kid," she prayed, squinting through the sparkle of rain in her headlights on the pitch-black road. At first, she didn't see anything, then she spotted something large, black and hairy in the ditch to the right of the car—and a new fear was born. "Oh shit! Shit! Shit! Shit!"

She nearly slipped on the wet road, feeling it squish in her gold flip-flops as she reached past the open car door for her phone.

"Please don't let it be a werewolf." She grabbed her mace too, because what if God heard her prayers and she was dealing with a real injured wolf or some other dangerous animal? "Oh God, don't make me tell Des I killed someone from his pack. I do not need that this week."

She had to walk slow; her flip-flops were designed for a cute factor and had zero tractions. Literally the worse pair of shoes she could be wearing right now, and she was cursing her stupidity as she shined the light on her phone toward the body in the ditch.

"Hey!" She squinted, seeing the wagging of a tail. "Are you okay?"

His tail kept wagging. At least Amber assumed it was a he, but it was hard for her to tell in the dark when it was a wolf she was looking at. She raised her mace, worried again that it might be a real one instead of a werewolf.

But the tail thing was kinda creepy.

The wolf lifted his head, showing off teeth in a way that could have looked like he was smiling—which might have been cute, except a cold chill of terror spread down her spine and numbed her fingers.

Screw the wolf. She turned to leave—and another gasp of terror caught in her throat.

All she registered was a man coming at her, and Amber sprayed her mace automatically in a wild, sweeping arc, but the growl that echoed in those few seconds would haunt her forever.

She made a move to run, but before she could get far, the flip-flops betrayed her completely and she stumbled. A heartbeat later, a body slammed into hers, and Amber's vision went black from the agony when her forehead smacked hard on the pavement.

Dazed, stunned by the pain, Amber fought against the urge to throw up when she was forced onto her back. She blinked past the rain, feeling the warm blood from her forehead running into her eyes. She saw the shadows of a wolf change into a man, and then the fuzzy outlines of two faces haloed in the headlights.

"I think you killed her."

Amber *was* dying. She had to be. Her head felt cracked in two. She tried to roll over and get away, but someone fisted her hair before she could move, jerking so painfully she screamed.

"She's not dead." He tugged her head back harder, and she fought to break his hold, struggling and grunting. "Look at the fight in this one!"

"Hey, I thought Leroy said we weren't supposed to hurt her too badly," the other werewolf warned. "You know how fucking easy it is to kill 'em. We're always dealing with one of your damn human hunting accidents."

"Nah, watch, I got this new trick. Grab the rags and bungie cords from my bag."

Amber gasped when he wrapped a hand around her throat, kicking when her air was suddenly gone. The blood, rain and darkness made it almost impossible to make out much, but she saw the whites of the werewolf's eyes as he laughed sadistically while cutting off her air supply. She fought harder, clawing at his hands, trying to kick him in the balls, but he was so strong it was like fighting a statue.

Katie was right, Merl wasn't the worst—not even close.

It was the last thought Amber had before she felt the fight suddenly go out of her body. Her hands just stopped working without her permission. The rain glittering in the headlights faded away like stardust, and then...nothing.

It felt like a thousand years before Amber started to wake up. She struggled to move, but someone jerked her hair so hard, she tried to scream but couldn't.

The nightmare came back in a sickening rush.

Amber's entire body tensed with panic when she found herself choking. At first, she thought the hand was still around her throat, but she realized it was worse than that. A cloth of some kind was forcing her mouth open so wide her cheeks bulged and her jaw hurt.

Her hands were tied behind her back, and when she tried to kick, she discovered her legs were tied, too.

"Told ya she'd come back around." The one holding her hair pulled harder, turning her head, letting Amber spy the light from the trunk hood above her. "See, she likes it."

She was trapped in her own trunk, trying to get away from the disgusting coppery taste, but she couldn't. There was nowhere to go, and fighting was hurting her worse. She realized the werewolf was holding his bleeding wrist to the rag shoved in her mouth, soaking it with his blood, giving her so much she was drowning in it.

By some small miracle, the hold on her hair loosened, and he let her go, but she still couldn't move much. Her shoulders were already hurting from the way her arms were tied. In the beam of light from the trunk, she blinked to see a huge, blurry figure step back and look down at her.

A younger-looking werewolf came up next to the one who'd been holding her, studying Amber with a frown. "Rich, you better pull that rag out of her mouth soon. I don't think Leroy's gonna like that, and my ma said not to get caught up with your bullshit."

"Fuck your ma. If we pull the rag out, she'll be screaming all the way back." Rich reached forward and grabbed something behind Amber's head. "Help me finish tying her so she's not kicking in the trunk, and we'll stop for a burger on the way back."

Amber was still choking, trying not to swallow any more blood, when the two of them grabbed her once more. She struggled, not caring if they killed her when she was mute and half blind in the dark. It was worse than death. The younger werewolf held her down while Rich started wrapping a bungy cord around her head, trapping the blood-soaked rag in her mouth.

"Breathe in through your nose, whore, and you won't die."

He hooked the bungie cord together at the back of her head, and then started working on her, binding them together with a second cord, effectively hogtying her with horrifying efficiency.

"Wait and see, she'll be healed up and dripping wet by the time we get her to pack land." He laughed as he said it. "The last one I caught in Reno, man, I thought I fucking killed her before I threw her in the trunk, but a little blood for the ride back and she started begging the second we pulled the gag out of her mouth. Best human hunting trick *ever*. A cheetah in Freeport taught it to me."

Rich slammed the hood, plunging Amber into darkness. For several seconds she had to lie there and fight to breathe through her nose. Then the car started, and she got even more terrified, as if that was possible.

No one would be able to find her.

There were going to take her God knows where and do God knows what with her. This was it. She was going to die in the worst way possible, and she hadn't done a thing with her life. Not one thing.

Amber tried to roll over, attempting to get on her stomach so she wouldn't have to swallow any more, but the way he had her arms and hands bound together behind her back made it impossible. It was a cruel, agonizing position to leave her in, but that was probably the point. She could barely move.

Sick bastards.

She found herself praying they were some of Desmon's wolves, that he would somehow how find out and show up before something worse happened, but she suspected they weren't, and he was out in the woods somewhere chasing after his own pack.

What if she ran out of time?

What would happen when the bloodlust grabbed her without Desmon to help her?

Every part of her hurt, and there was no way to get away from the blood, it was everywhere, in her mouth, her nose, running down the sides of her cheeks.

She started working on the zip-ties holding her wrists together instead, frantically trying to somehow loosen them. Maybe she could punch out one of the taillights and get someone's attention. But the werewolf tied her viciously tight, so much it was cutting off her circulation. She couldn't even feel her feet.

Never in her entire life had she ever been so powerless. So weak.

The pulse of fear throbbed through every fiber of her body. In that moment, she hoped to God they *did* turn her into a werewolf, because she wanted rip every last one of them apart.

The fury rose up the back of her neck, hot and seductive, as she thought about biting into them, utterly destroying them and bathing in their blood when she was done. The heat spread everywhere, all over her body in a warm, compelling wave, turning her fury into something far more sinister.

God, no, please.

Amber started mentally praying when her breathing fell shallow in primal desperation. Her muscles seized next, and she found herself thinking of Desmon. She needed him there to distract her. She was clinging to something, anything, to make her less terrified.

12

The shrill ring of a cell phone echoed in the woods, sounding completely out of place in the peaceful quiet of nature. Desmon stopped his patrol on the edge of the Goodwin boarder and turned his head, growling and showing his teeth.

Irritated, he transformed and stood naked in the woods, wearing Miles's old Alliance harness that was too loose in wolf form and too tight in human form.

He pulled the phone off the clip on his side. It had been raining all night, and he had to fight to slip the phone out of the waterproof case while he walked over to a tree, hoping for shelter. He was about to start growling at whoever called him, when he saw it was Katie.

He answered it quickly, forgetting about the need to hide his phone from the rain. "What's wrong?"

"Hey." Katie sounded nervous. "Have you seen Amber?"

"It's the full moon. I'm in the woods, Katie." Fear gripped Desmon, tightening his chest. "Why would I have seen her?"

"She left for ice cream a couple of hours ago and she's not back." Her voice was shaking. "And Bea told me something—"

Desmon let out a low growl.

"Come on, you have to promise to stay calm, 'cause I'm kinda breaking sister code by telling you this."

"*What is it?*" Desmon started running in the direction of the clearing, but he was still at least a half mile away from the Quick Mart. "Is Amber in danger?"

"Maybe. She's not answering her phone. I didn't know what else to do," Katie choked. "And Bea just told me they ran into Gary Goodwin at a store this afternoon. He was being really creepy around Amber, sniffing her, saying weird shit."

"She went into neutral territory while she was unprotected and unmated?" Desmon stopped running to process the shiver of raw horror that rolled down his spine. "I told her to stay on pack land. She had my scent on her. That's a red fucking flag to weres everywhere."

"She's still new at this," Katie whispered nervously. "She doesn't know how dangerous outside weres are. She never believes me when I tell her Merl kept us safe from them. Gary told her to head out to the border and spy on you for the running. What if Amber fell for it?" Katie asked in panic. "She could've gotten curious and decided to stop."

"She wouldn't do that." Desmon was sure of it, even as his breathing fell shallow with fear. "She's not that naive."

"Well, she's not back! It's raining. Maybe she got into a wreck on the mountain. Something's happened to her."

"I'm coming, Katie. I'm heading your way. Keep trying to get ahold of her," Desmon barked, fighting down the beast in him that came roaring to life. "Call me back the second you hear something."

He hung up and called Jazz, who answered on the first ring because he was forced to stay in human form while in town.

"God, I can't keep track of these girls. They're all over the place. Why are you huffing in my ear? Are you running?"

"I think my mate's in danger." Desmon was still racing toward the clearing, but he knew he needed backup before he completely lost control of himself. "You have to hold the pack until I find her."

"What?" Jazz's voice changed, becoming suddenly sharp and serious.

"Katie called me; Amber's missing, and Katie said Gary Goodwin was sniffing her at a store today." The hair on Desmon's arms and face grew long, and his voice became completely inhuman. "They know she's mine!"

"Okay, Desmon, listen to me, we'll find her. You need to try and stay calm—"

Desmon snarled into the phone in response, hearing it crack in his grip. He pulled back to look at it, seeing the glass was shattered, and roared again.

"Meet me at Amber's house!" Desmon managed to choke out before he lost his ability to speak completely.

He couldn't afford to abandon his phone now, and he had to fight to get it back in the waterproof case. As soon as he got it clipped on Miles's harness, Desmon shifted and let out a long howl of warning to his wolves, because he was still responsible for them and the obligation went down to his bones.

With the throb of fear still pounding through his veins in his wolf form, Desmon took off toward the clearing at full speed. It wasn't like him to abandon them—but he had priorities, and Amber would always be his number one.

"Whew, smell her."

Amber blinked when the trunk opened, completely dazed, because everything looked...weird. Details were sharper and more vivid, and for a moment, the horrible, all-consuming nightmare of fear and desire paused. It was still dark outside. The dim beam from the hood was the only light, but she could see clearer than if it was mid-day.

"Fuck." A tall, well-dressed man with short dark hair and broad shoulders groaned like he was in pain and cupped a hand to his face. "What the hell did you do to her, Rich?"

Amber tilted her head back, still blinking to adjust to the vibrant colors and painful throb between her legs. Her entire body felt hot. Every muscle was tense with a powerful, pulsing energy so overwhelming, it made her want to crawl out of her skin.

"I had to give her a little blood." Rich came into view, looking small and more subservient next to the other wolf. "She hit her head when we caught her, and you said to keep this one extra healthy since she's Nightwind bait."

"You had one fucking job—the *easiest* job. Literally the pup could've done it without you. How does this shit always happen with you?"

"Sorry, Alpha," Rich muttered like it was a habit.

The taller werewolf grabbed Amber's head, unhooked and unwrapped the bungie cord. He tossed it aside, and she didn't have time to enjoy the small freedom before he fisted Amber's hair in a way that made it obvious, he didn't care about her pain any more than the other wolf did.

"A little blood?" The alpha wolf squeezed her cheeks with his other hand before she could try to somehow push the rag out of her mouth. "This thing's soaked. I told you the last time, this is too much!"

"I thought she might die, and since you needed her for the Nightwind raid—"

"I can't even tell if she's the right one, her scent's too strong now." The larger werewolf cut him off and sniffed Amber closer. "I think she's already half turned. This is more than bloodlust, this is fucked-up were-zombie lust."

"The cheetah in Freeport said he keeps his catches for months like this, and they never turn on him," Rich complained, sounding like a petulant child. "He just feeds 'em blood like that when he's done playing with them, and they heal up. Cats play with their catches for months, years sometimes. That's why they know this stuff. He says it just keeps 'em feisty."

"Yeah, I bet it does." The alpha suddenly backhanded Rich without warning, making the smaller wolf stumble. "Asshole! He's selling them in the underground. He's keeping them blood-drunk and renting them out. It's a huge fucking problem right now. The Alliance is slitting throats over it. *This* is why I keep telling you to stop talking to these weird shifters when you're hunting. They give you bad ideas."

Rich shrugged. "I think he was trying to help."

"Remember that time you shot yourself in the foot with a silver bullet because that city wolf told you drinking orange juice made you immune? They fuck with you on purpose."

"I know," Rich agreed, sounding disappointed. "But I don't think that's true this time. 'Cause, the human I caught in Reno wasn't moving, and—"

"Goddamn, Rich." The alpha rubbed a hand over his face, like he couldn't believe what he was hearing. "Let me try to explain this. I give you permission to catch a couple humans a month because we're not city wolves out here. Pack wolves still need to hunt and play around a little, and the Alliance *knows* that. As long as it doesn't show up on the news, they don't give a shit about a few humans disappearing in the woods. We eat what we catch. No money changes hands. We don't have a collection in the basement. It's for *entertainment only*. But this right here? It has 'dealer' written all over it. Any shifter walking by can smell her, and I'm not getting executed for your dumb ass!"

"We'll just get rid of her after a couple of days like we did with Reno," Rich grumbled. "No one will know. Who's going to smell her out here?"

Rather than respond, the alpha turned his attention back on Amber. His pupils dilated while he looked at her, and she couldn't hold back the low, vicious sound that rumbled from the center of her chest.

Even as sexually pent up as she was, burning up so bad she felt like she'd die from it, she hated this wolf—she'd never be that desperate.

"Look at her, growling at me." He caught Amber's hair, holding her head while she kept grunting and growling to break away. "Fuck, she's making my dick hurt. Your cheetah buddy is probably making a fortune if he's found a way to keep them ripe like this for months." His voice had a low growl to it, like he was becoming more animal than man. "I can just imagine what she's doing to *you*. I bet you wanna start humping furniture. You and every male in this pack."

Without warning, he let go of Amber and grabbed Rich, who let out a dog-like whimper. The alpha bent Rich over the trunk and pressed his face against his face against the floorboard, holding him there.

"Stay," the alpha growled, and Rich stopped struggling, but kept breathing hard with his face pinned against the floorboard in front of Amber. "You wanna make her smell like that? Fine. Thanks to you, no one's allowed to even *look* at her until Desmon Nightwind's head is on my doorstep. The pack gets to suffer until then, and I'm gonna make sure they all know it's *your* fault."

Rich was huffing and growling, but he let himself be pinned down rather than fight, and grunted, "Yes, Alpha."

Obviously satisfied, or easily bored, the alpha wolf stepped back, and shoved Rich at the same time, making him fall into the mud.

The alpha turned to Amber once more and folded his arms, contemplating her in the open trunk. "She's cute," he mused thoughtfully. "Shame to eat her, but we sure as hell can't keep her smelling like that."

Amber growled when he suddenly reached out and fisted her hair again.

"Don't growl at me—I like it," the alpha wolf snapped when she tried to tug out of his hold.

He showed off long, sharp teeth, and snarled at her in warning, before he raised his other hand and bit viciously into his own wrist. He made a show of tearing away the flesh with a gush of blood, like the pain of it didn't even faze him.

Amber fought desperately to turn her head, but he held her tighter as he forced his wrist to the bleeding rag in her mouth.

She kept struggling, but there was nowhere to go as the alpha wolf tilted her head back so it was easier for the blood to go down her throat. She could feel her heartbeat reverberating in her ears so loud it was deafening. The fury rolled under the surface, but Amber could only narrow her eyes at him while he poisoned her.

"You're glaring at me, but I'm doing you a favor. Alpha blood will keep *anything* alive." The alpha's pupils dilated more, making him look completely primitive when she was forced to start swallowing convulsively. "There she goes. That's it, pet." He smiled encouragingly, his wolf teeth long and deadly. "She'll survive getting the growl fucked out of her now."

Underneath the hard, throbbing pulse of anger, Amber knew it was already done. No matter what happened, her old life was over, and she mourned more than she thought she would. Everything got blurry when tears of fury, powerlessness, rolled down her cheeks.

Neither of them noticed.

The alpha wolf finally stopped holding his wrist to her mouth and licked the bleeding wound, sucking on it as he stared down at Amber as though proud of himself.

"Take a picture. I'll send it to Gary and find out if she's the right one. If she is, I'll call the Nightwinds—'cause too bad for them, she's *ours* now. I might even keep her at my place for a few weeks."

The alpha wolf leaned over once more, this time pushing Amber's hair from her face like he was trying to make her features more visible. "I heard one of their pack enforcers, Jason, started keeping a human like she's his mate but he won't change her. He has her in his house, sleeping in his bed, sniffing her ass every night like he wouldn't eat her if he was hungry, and Desmon lets him do it."

He squeezed Amber's cheeks and smiled, showing off still sharp wolf teeth. "But you don't have to worry about that now, do you, pet? You're too cute to eat, huh? Growling at me." He forced the rag deeper into her mouth with his thumb and caressed her bottom lip. "I'll let you thank me later."

"Yeah," Rich agreed distantly, his voice sounding dazed with lust while he blinded Amber with the light from his phone and snapped pictures. The alpha held her head, while Rich leaned in to get a close-up. "She already smells spicier."

"Too bad you won't get a taste. Rule still stands. You're still not allowed to fuck any of our bitches. We don't need any more of *you* in this pack."

The alpha stood back and slammed the trunk shut again, but Amber could still hear clearly, despite being plunged back into darkness.

"Jesus, don't look so fucking sad, Rich. It's not totally your fault. No one should've let your father fuck your mother, either. That's our fault. Couple weeks, I'll let you off pack land again, you can go pay your buddy in Reno for a good time with one of his blood-drunk humans. You won't die. Maybe if we get Jazz, I'll let you watch us break her in until Desmon shows up."

"Thank you, Alpha," Rich said quickly. "We'll get him."

"Sure." Footsteps walked away, sloshing in the mud. "You've got guard duty. You or any other male in this pack touches one hair on her fucking head before I say so, and you're never getting off pack land to hunt. Don't think I won't smell it if you decide to start toying with her, 'cause you know I will."

"I won't."

"Keep the trunk *shut*, Rich. I'm not kidding. Don't be sniffing after her. Let her marinate for a couple more hours. Things go bad, and we can still catch some of the younger Nightwind males with her scent. I might need you to drive her to a different location. If I call you, and you don't answer—"

"I'll answer, Alpha," Rich promised quickly, his voice still shaky. "I will."

"Okay, text me those pictures."

It was quiet after that, with the sound of the footsteps drifting farther and farther away. Amber was still trying to breathe through her nose. In those moments, she knew she sounded exactly like what they were turning her into—a trapped animal, huffing and growling as she searched desperately for an escape.

She wasn't scared, she was angry, and she channeled all that anger into biting on the rag in her mouth as her heartbeat seemed to get louder and louder in the darkness of the car.

Rather than try to get away from the blood, she worked on drinking more of it in a desperate bid for escape. She had no idea how to change into a werewolf, but knew she had to try. It was her only chance. If she changed, maybe she could run into the woods and find Desmon. It was a long shot, but it was the only thing she could think of.

Frantically, she bit harder, trying to swallow more of the blood, all the while imagining being a wolf. Maybe it was a mind-over-matter thing. She kept trying to think of Desmon, and her sisters, but the reason why she wanted to shift started to fade behind the desperation.

She struggled to slip her hands past the zip-tie, leaving her wrists sticky with blood. She continued to suck on the rag in her mouth, biting at it, taking out her frustrations on it, but the pulse in her head kept getting louder.

Deafening.

It was making the ache between her legs worse and worse, until it became the bigger problem. The stifling heat in the trunk started to become unbearable, making her clothes stick to her as they coated her body like a second skin.

Slowly, as she struggled to free herself, the reason why she was angry started to slip away. She started shifting and fighting for a different reason, desperate for an escape from the warmth in the trunk. She would do *anything* for relief from the pounding between her legs. Every movement that caused the lace of her bra to brush her tingling nipples made the pressure coil tighter, until Amber was shaking with repressed need, until all her clothes hurt her skin.

The way her hands were tied was sheer hell. She didn't even remember what she was fighting for. She just knew she needed the throbbing to stop. Not being able to move made need crawl under her skin and snake into her brain, scorching her along the way.

She tried to kick at the trunk, hoping he'd let her out. She'd beg if she had to, she was that desperate, but her arms and legs were still bound together with the bungie cord.

Amber couldn't do anything to make it stop.

Nothing.

Abandoning her plan of changing into a wolf, she tried to push the rag out of her mouth with her tongue, but she couldn't get it out. The harder and faster her heartbeat pounded in her ears, the more the blood seemed to burn her tongue. She wanted to get away from it, to run a thousand miles and never have it touch her again. It made her feel horrible and dirty.

And hot.

Rich beat the trunk with his fist. "The more you move around like that, the worse you're making it on both of us."

She started growling and struggling in earnest, desperate for attention. She tried to make as much noise as she could, because she needed out of the darkness. She needed...

Amber moaned and arched her hips, shifting impatiently.

"I said stop wiggling!" A fist hit the hood once more, before his voice dropped to a low grumble. "Fucking Leroy. Hope Desmon eats him. I got bitches in Reno, plenty of 'em." He pounded the hood once more. "You don't want me to open this trunk. I'll make it worth the punishment, I promise!"

13

The rain made everything a thousand times worse.

Desmon knew tracking Amber's scent would be nearly impossible. The harder the rain fell, the more hope of picking up her scent washed away, and his wolf was half insane by the time he got to Amber's house.

Amber's sister Katie was sitting on the porch waiting for him, smelling of fear so strongly, even the rain couldn't hide it. She jumped up as Desmon shifted at the bottom step.

"Here, they're Merl's." Katie tossed a pair of sweatpants at Desmon, her gaze averted from his naked form as she reminded him, "Bea's here."

Desmon was too terrified to do anything more than step into the sweats Katie handed him. The material was difficult, because Desmon was dripping wet. He fought not to rip them apart in a fit of anger. His hands were shaking, his braided hair heavy against his back as he fought to find some semblance of control.

"You think the Goodwins have her?" Katie asked in a low, fearful voice while Desmon moved under the cover of the porch to make dressing easier. "You think—"

"Be quiet about that." Desmon sounded harsher than he wanted to. He couldn't stop thinking about Amber at the mercy of the Goodwins, and it was making it hard for him to fully hold his human form. "Tell me what happened."

"She left to get ice cream from the store, that's it," Katie said in a rush. "And we can't get ahold of her. We've called her a million times. She's not answering."

"Can you track her phone?"

Katie shook her head quickly. "No."

"Her laptop." Desmon's breathing was still rough as he silently fought the battle to turn off his wolf side so he could problem solve through human issues. "Can you get into it and log into her phone that way?"

"Maybe." Katie turned toward the door. "I'll go check."

"I'll wait out here." Desmon knew he was on the edge of losing control, so he didn't trust himself around humans, but especially Amber's youngest sister. "Keep Bea inside."

Katie met his gaze for one long moment, and then nodded like she understood. She went back in the house to search Amber's computer for information, but Desmon couldn't sit on the steps and wait. Instead he paced in the rain, back and forth, knowing he was losing the battle against his baser nature, even if he was still holding human form. Every muscle in his body was tense as he fought down the wolf howling under the surface for him to shift and run headlong into Goodwin territory.

The problem was, he didn't know where she was, and it would be easy for any wolf to get killed in Goodwin territory, because like it or not, Leroy Goodwin and his brother Gary were formidable alphas with a strong pack behind them.

He wanted to rip off the harness as an outlet, but he kept it on, and instead stepped under the cover of the porch as the need to fight raged a war with the images of what the Goodwins would do to a human like Amber. He pulled the .45 out of its case on Miles's harness, dropped the magazine to check the bullets, and then racked the slide to make sure everything was working smoothly.

It was un-shifter-like to fight with weapons, but he didn't give a fuck.

He'd shoot a hundred wolves to rescue his angel.

His breathing became more ragged, and he was finally losing his ability to stay fully human when a van came speeding onto the muddy patch in front of the yard.

Jazz sprang out from the driver's side and shouted to the females in the back, "Stay here!"

Desmon snarled at his best friend when Jazz came rushing at him, but the sound was more wounded than furious.

Jazz grabbed Desmon and half-dragged him around to the side of the house, away from the open front door. "You can't be near the humans. Her sisters—"

Something about that only compounded the fear, crippling Desmon to the point that he fell to his knees in the mud, desperate and overwhelmed. He half-shifted out of necessity, the hair long on his arms and face.

"If they have her..." He felt lost already, the images in the back of his mind making him physically ill. "We'll never find her. There'll be nothing left."

The look on Jazz's face was savage, haunted in the dark shadows and misty rain from the porch lights. They had never found Jazz's mate, and though they never talked about it, everyone knew why.

"Listen to me, Des." Jazz fell down into the mud with Desmon and looked him dead in the eye. "We're going to find her. Even if we have to rip apart the Goodwins wolf by wolf."

"By then—" Desmon shook his head, remembering what his mother had gone through at the hands of Albert, and she'd been a wolf at the time. "What will they have done to her?"

"Whatever it is, you'll help her heal." Jazz's voice was more wolf growl than human. "I'll fight to the death to keep you from losing your mate."

"I will, too."

Desmon looked up, seeing Miles coming around the corner with Jason in tow. His cousin was dressed in military combat wear, with camouflage pants and his brown hunting vest. Like Desmon, Miles's hair was braided. He held a rifle in his hand that told the world he was ready to fight. In stark contrast, Jason wore only sweatpants like Desmon. Bare-chested and barefoot, he was there to fight too—only he preferred fur.

"You know we got your back, Des," Jason assured him.

Desmon hadn't even heard them get here, which should have scared him, but he was past that. As much as he appreciated his pack being there, it felt like the guilt was ripping up his insides.

"You were right," Desmon confessed to his cousin, his voice still the growl of a wolf, rather than the smooth timber of a man. "I should've stayed with my mate tonight."

"I tracked her phone!" Katie came running around the corner before Miles could answer, blonde hair clinging to her face and neck in the rain. Miles stepped in her way, blocking her from Desmon and Jazz, who were both still kneeling in the mud, but that didn't stop her. "S-She's on Curly Road, but her dot isn't moving, and—"

Katie stopped talking when Jazz's phone started ringing.

Jazz leaned back and reached into his jeans pocket for his phone. "It's probably one of the other enforcers. I sent out a group text. Jason was just the first to show up since he doesn't run for the full moon."

But Jazz paled when he stared at the screen. He glanced up at Miles, who was still standing in front of Katie, and the two of them must have silently communicated something.

Jazz suddenly jumped up and ran toward the woods at the back of the house. At the same time, Miles sprang forward, tackling Desmon to the ground just when he would've run after Jazz.

Even from a distance, Desmon could hear the growl of Leroy Goodwin's voice from Jazz's phone, but the actual words were lost as Miles fought him rather than let him go. He heard Jason drag Katie back inside over the snarls and growls Desmon only dimly realized were coming from him, as he and Miles rolled in the mud.

Miles fought better in skin than Desmon did, he was more comfortable with it these days. Even half-transformed, Desmon couldn't get away from him, and when he tried to lash out, the mud made Miles too slippery.

The terror made him vicious, and somewhere in the back of his mind, he felt his father's disappointment when he shifted completely and sank his teeth hard into Mile's forearm.

Miles shouted in shock, because Desmon had never done that. No matter how pissed off he was, he'd never attacked his cousin in fur since Miles's accident—it wasn't fair—but his wolf didn't give a fuck.

Desmon used his shock to slip out from under Miles, and then shifted back to human form, fighting with the sweatpants that got tangled when he was a man once more. Miles made a move to grab him again but Desmon took off, running at Jazz.

Jazz stood his ground in the rain, the phone held to his ear as Desmon barreled at him. He already knew the Goodwins had her. He'd known it the second he heard the echo of Leroy's voice from Jazz's phone. Desmon wasn't sure what he was going to do to Jazz when he got to him, his best friend—and the man who now knew if Amber was already dead.

Maybe Desmon would've tackled and fought him until he told him the truth—but the way Jazz's hand dropped, the phone still tight in his grip as he stared at Desmon, drained all the fight out of him.

A howl of wounded horror and rage came from the center of his chest, and he dropped right there in the mud on Amber's property.

Desmon knew right then, if Amber was gone, he was done, even at the risk of abandoning his pack. Before, protecting them had been enough. This time it wouldn't be—Desmon was sure of it.

"She's not dead," Jazz whispered, but the grim tone of his voice made it sound like she might as well be when he walked over to Desmon.

Desmon blinked through the rain to look up at him, a small glimmer of hope bursting to life in the center of his chest.

Jazz swallowed hard. "Leroy changed her."

Desmon must've heard him wrong. "*What?*"

"Some bullshit story about an accident on the road. He claims he did it to save her life." Jazz choked as he said it. "He already emailed a notice to the Alliance saying she's part of his pack now."

Desmon jumped to his feet, still in human form. "She's my *mate*. I tasted her. Nature says she belongs to *me*. Fuck the Alliance!"

"You're not *mated* though," Jazz reminded him with a wince. "It's his blood changing her. Technically, she's under his protection, unless she can find a mate outside his pack. It's against the law to go into someone else's territory and take one of their females to mate by force. You know damn well he's going to lie and accuse you of just that if you rescue Amber. He's been spoiling for a fight for years, trying to make us look like we're the aggressors. He contacted the damn Alliance to make them think this was a mercy change. Total fucking bullshit. We *know* he took her. But that's the info he gave. You go after Amber, our entire pack will pay for it."

"He's right. It'll be war if you get her now." Miles's voice came from behind them. "And we'll be the ones guilty of starting it. Unless she's off their pack land when you mate her—"

"Which she won't be." Jazz's voice was edged with ice. "There's no way Leroy's letting her close enough to the borders to reach our territory."

"I'll go rogue to get her back. You keep the pack," Desmon decided for all of them, because Amber was alive, and suffering through the change in the center of the Goodwins. Even five seconds in their clutches felt like too long. "Now the war's with me and I'm the only one guilty. She's my mate. I'll stand trial if I have to."

It was Desmon's job to protect his mate. It was a rule of nature, one they all respected and understood completely.

Still, Jazz shook his head. "We need a better plan."

"We don't have time!" Desmon gestured to the direction of Goodwin territory. "I get my mate back. I deal with the consequences. That's it!"

"You can't run into the center of Goodwin territory by yourself! You know this is a trap. They'll be waiting for you," Jazz shouted at him. "It's suicide!"

"Not if I go with him," Miles cut in. "We slip in, slip out. The rain will mess with their noses. They can't track well if they can't smell. That's their only magic trick. We'll have an advantage."

"It's not enough," Jazz argued frantically. "It's way too much to risk!"

"Fuck the risk!" Desmon growled at him. "My wolf knows she's mine. You'll have to put me down if we don't do this."

"If you do this, you'll be putting *yourself* down, and Miles along with you," Jazz argued. "If I'm going to agree, I need a five-minute fucking plan before we throw you both to the Goodwins. If your wolf's got you so nuts you can't see that, then you're just going to have to trust that I'm right about this—because if she's really your mate, you'll be dooming her, too, by running into a trap and getting yourself killed. Remember, she's a wolf now. She won't survive losing you, either. Is that something you want to risk?"

"Amber has Leroy Goodwin's blood running through her veins right now—changing her!" Desmon's voice was completely inhuman, and it was only his lifelong trust in and friendship with Jazz that allowed him to agree. "You got three minutes to come up with a plan. Starting now."

14

"Rich," Amber called out in a singsong voice. "Open the trunk."

"I said no." Rich was clearly miserable, because Amber had been toying with him for a while. "Alpha'll make it horrible. It's not worth it. I got bitches in Reno better than this one." It sounded more like he was talking to himself than Amber, and he hit the hood of the trunk for what had to be the thousandth time. "Now shut your fucking trap."

Amber had gotten free from her bindings a while ago. Between one flash and the next, something happened, sharp teeth and fur, and she'd been able to suddenly wiggle free.

"Just let me taste you." Amber's voice was low, husky with the rasp of need. "They can't smell that, can they, if we just play around a little?"

"It *is* raining." Rich sounded unsure. "If I pull out before—" The ring of a phone cut him off, and he cursed. The weight of the car shifted like he was moving to get it out of his pocket. "Hey, Alpha, I haven't fucked her."

"Are you sure? Cause it sounds like you're planning on it...after I told you not to." The alpha's voice was clear and highly irritated through the phone, which was as strange as everything else. Amber heard it in a way that was foreign as he growled, "I'm sending Gary your way. The Nightwinds are attacking on the north border, right where we wanted them, but there's a lot of them. Something about that makes me nervous. Desmon wants this one more than I thought if he's willing to lose pack wolves and risk the Alliance coming down on him. This is more than full moon entertainment now, and you know you're my weak link, Rich. You could fuck it all up."

"I know, Alpha," Rich whispered despondently.

"Stay in the south end until Gary gets there. I have enforcers surrounding the whole area. You have one job in this pack, and you know you're in danger of losing it. No more humans for you. *You'll* be our pack entertainment if this goes bad. So sit there on the trunk and don't move for anything. You're not fighting. You're just *sitting*. It's an easy fucking job. Can you do that?"

"Yes, Alpha, and I was thinking—"

The phone clicked off before Rich could finish, meaning the alpha hung up without a goodbye. Not all that shocking. Rich started to kick the trunk harder, over and over, letting Amber know it was a stress outlet.

She sensed his fear.

It almost felt like she could smell it as a new scent flooded into the trunk from above, bitter, unpleasant, like the burn of battery acid...and it gave her an idea.

"He's going to see you opened the trunk when he gets here," Amber called out in the same sultry voice. "He'll know you were bad."

"I didn't!" Rich shouted, sounding suddenly terrified. "I wasn't!"

"How can you prove it, though?" Amber kicked the trunk pointedly, using the heels of her bare feet. "I'm not tied up anymore, Richie Boy. How'd I do that if you didn't let me out?"

"Oh no." Rich groaned in panic. "Fuck!"

He jumped down, and a pulse of excitement started throbbing through Amber's body at the thought of being free. He couldn't possibly be *that* stupid...

But he was, because the hood popped open in the next second.

She rolled onto her back, spreading out over the bungie cords as she licked her bloody lips and cupped her tits. Rich's gaze followed her hands obediently, before he leaned down to smell her with a low, drunken groan.

In a flash, it happened, and Amber lashed out with a furious snarl, sinking sharp teeth into Rich's neck.

This time she savored the heady, dark taste of blood on her tongue as she clenched down harder, feeling the deadly strength of her jaws. Rich's pained yell turned into a whinny screech of agony when he shifted, and the two of them fell to the ground.

He was the one who'd held her back from her mate, no matter how many times she'd begged him to open the trunk. She wanted him to die, but more than that—she needed Desmon.

Thinking his name made her taste the blood in a different way, and she noticed the Goodwin alpha's tang all over again. Even under the taste of Rich, Leroy was still in her mouth and sticky on her skin. She felt like his blood was everywhere, tainting her.

She let go of Rich when the smells hit her next, and it was a thousand times worse, crushing in on her from all sides. She couldn't tell the difference between them, not when there were so many.

Scared, disoriented, she fought to free herself from the clothes, ripping at them with her teeth, hating them. She moved to break free when Rich, now a brown wolf, caught her tail with his teeth. She snarled and snapped at him, the terror making her vicious enough that Rich jumped back with another yelp.

Amber took off running after that, not bothering to look behind her. She followed the sound of the water, wanting to be clean, desperate to have all the scents off her.

Everything felt broken.

It all smelled wrong. She wasn't sure why she knew it, but she did.

She needed her mate.

Her body ached, but only Desmon would do, other males made her feel horribly uncomfortable to the point that she felt sick.

Finally, she stopped to sit in the mud and rain, staring at her paws, dirty and wet. Her pale fur was stained pink in places, the scent of it still choking her.

Amber didn't have paws—she had hands.

The second she thought it, she found herself kneeling naked in the middle of the forest, and it wasn't an improvement. She got shakily to her feet, too overwhelmed to worry about her lack of clothing.

It felt like her smallest problem, especially when she couldn't figure out how to turn back into a wolf, even though she could still hear like one. The howls in the distance resonated like whispers far inside her ears. The gust of the wind through the leaves haunted her, but the rush of water flowing downstream called out. She started stumbling through the woods, following the sound of the river.

Being in human form was awful. The panic was overwhelming, making her feel vulnerable. Too many thoughts swirled around in her mind when only two things really mattered, getting these other males' scents off her and finding Desmon.

The light and shadows looked strange. The scents were still too weird, too different than they were when she was human. She relied on her ears, the echo of water rushing over rocks leading her like salvation, and she kept going, even when the howls sounded closer and the rustle of leaves seemed to change. Her senses told her something was off.

She took off, feeling a weird pop in her bones when the whispers of the forest turned to growls behind her. It got easier for her once more, and Amber started running hard. It wasn't until she took a left, still desperate for the river, that she glanced over her shoulder, seeing the blur of her own white tail—before something jumped out of the trees at her.

Amber snarled and snapped when she was suddenly rolling in the mud, but this wolf was different than Rich. He didn't cower when she bit him. He bit back, sharp teeth and powerful jaws crushing down on her shoulder when he jumped on her.

Amber's yelp of agony turned into a scream of pain when she was suddenly in human form once more. Flat on her face on the forest floor, with wolf teeth buried in tender flesh, she fought to get away from him, but then he was human, too. He wrapped a forearm around her throat from behind, getting her in a choke hold before she could get away.

"Stop fighting, and I'll give you what you want. Leroy told me you were alpha feisty, but I'm one, too. You'll like how I do it." He breathed against her ear. "You want me to fuck you, huh? Give you a little taste before later?"

Amber struggled harder.

"Hey!" He fisted her hair, jerking her head back. "I said I'd give it to you now."

"Go suck a bag of dicks!" Amber growled low and deep in her chest, and then flashed her teeth in the darkness when she saw it was Gary, the weirdo from town. "Give it to yourself! You disgust me!"

"Sure." He snorted like her words meant nothing. "You'll be thanking me once you have a thick one in you, begging for more like the rest of them. We already know you like shifter dick, and trust me, Goodwin alpha's better than Nightwind alpha any day of the week."

Fear washed over her, a blanket of horror even the wild, fearless new side of her couldn't resist when she found herself pinned down by this naked Goodwin. She yelped and cried out, flashing between wolf and human; it was agonizing on her bones and her muscles. Gary started cursing, trying to hold her down while she fought to free herself before he could enter her.

She managed to slip away for a few seconds, scampering in the mud in human form, but she was dragged back by her hair as Gary huffed, "Look at this, a brand-new bitch in bloodlust, not wanting it. You know what that means, don't you? You have specific tastes, sweetheart, 'cause we both know you're desperate for it. I can smell it. I think you have a mate."

The harder she wrestled to get away, the more amused he seemed to become, until Amber found herself flat on her back with Gary straddled over her. He forced both her hands over her head, holding her there while she snarled and panted like a feral animal.

She tried to turn back into a wolf, desperate for her teeth, but she wasn't sure how she had actually been doing it. The smell of him was making her genuinely ill, and she finally gave up, chest heaving, and turned her head away to get a clear breath of air.

"Okay, which one is it?" Gary's hold on her wrists was bruising. His strength terrifying. "I smelled Desmon on you in town. I figured it was a hookup, a little weekend human to get sticky with since he's so sentimental about them, but maybe that's not it. If you're fucking in the pack, it could've been any of them. Did he share you with Jazz, too? Did the two of them stop loving each *other* long enough to finally put a female between them? They probably keep you there every night, don't they?

"Or Miles. Maybe you had a little Nightwind sandwich for dinner last night." He leaned down and sniffed her again. "And your scent is sexy as hell, with that little extra alpha-bitch bite. I'm gonna love fucking you while he watches, but I don't think I wanna wait until later. If *you're* going this crazy, I want to see what *he* does when he smells me all over you."

He kissed her neck, and she gagged, wanting to sink into the earth to get away from him. He just laughed as she kept her head turned away, breathing through her mouth to hide from his scent, but it wasn't helping much.

She smelled it first, like a rush of fresh air, spicy and warm. For one moment, all the insanity seemed to still as she turned her head to look through the dark trees sparkling with life under her night vision.

If Gary had been paying attention, he might have noticed the change in her. Amber was still staring out to the woods, waiting for him, when a huge black wolf leapt out of the darkness, knocking Gary off her.

15

*A*mber felt the scrape of claws against her skin when the two of them rolled into the woods in a spray of fur and blood.

Though he was in wolf form, she knew it was Desmon. She recognized him, and even if she hadn't, she could feel him on every level, but it didn't calm her down. The sounds from the fight were vicious, the snarling, chilling battle of two dangerous canines. It was hard to see who was winning, but the combat was different than she'd seen with Jazz earlier. It was blatant in the first few seconds that the two of them were desperate to kill each other.

Amber started pacing in front of the two males fighting, feeling anxious, growling, wanting to help her mate, but not knowing how.

Then Gary shifted to his human form and grabbed Desmon, throwing him against the large tree next to him, making the wood splinter from the impact of Desmon's furry body.

When Desmon landed, a huge, motionless black wolf, Amber moved without thought, jumping at Gary when he changed back to attack Desmon with wolf teeth, but someone caught her before she could help her mate.

She immediately started fighting to get free from the stranger, to break out of the human arms wrapped around her, but he was too strong, his grip too powerful as he carried her away from Desmon.

Amber turned into a snarling, frantic beast, clawing at his arms with her paws, alternating between whining and growling as he stormed through the forest. He was talking to her, but she couldn't register what he was saying, aside from his cursing and struggling to hold on to her while she fought with all her might to break free. The worst part was the way he was holding her, halfway over his shoulder, his hand pulling the skin of her neck to the point that she could barely breathe. It was making it impossible for her to bite him—like he knew how to keep an angry wolf tame.

It would be easier if she could turn back into a human and break away like that, but same as before, she wasn't sure how to do it. The fear made it seem impossible, and the farther away she got from Desmon, the more blindingly panicked she became, because this guy was the strongest, scariest one yet. His hold was like steel, but she had to get away from him to save Desmon—*she had to*—like she needed air.

"Goddamn it, you've got a mean wolf, like down-to-your-fucking-core nasty!" The stranger stormed right into the river, sinking up to his knees. "You and Desmon should be perfect for each other. His wolf's an asshole, too."

Amber sucked in a sharp breath when he dropped her in the cold water. For one violent moment, it stole all her breath, and then she broke through the surface, coughing and wheezing. Her hair was in her face, blinding her, and she flipped it back, realizing she was human again.

That was the only thought she had before she started toward the shore, but he caught her left hand.

"Don't touch me!" Amber swung around and smacked him, hard, open palm against his cheek. She growled for good measure, showing off long teeth. "Stay away!"

"You're not listening." He spoke low, like he was trying to keep their location quiet, and he started blocking her hits when she went after him with intent, smacking his chest and arms, punching at the army vest he wore, because he wouldn't let her hand go. "Just look at me."

"Let me go!" She was still trying to hit him, but he blocked her over and over, never fighting back, just on the defensive, and it was extremely frustrating. When he finally caught her other wrist, holding them both trapped in his unforgiving grip, she tried to kick him in frustration because this man was like sticky paper. "I'll kill you!" She broke one hand away from his hold, making him curse when she smacked him again and screamed in his face, "If he dies, I'll fucking kill you!"

"He won't die," he growled at her in a low voice while still deflecting her blows. "I won't let that happen. I'm on *your* side. That's what I've been telling you."

Amber fell on the bank of the river, landing flat on her back as she glared up at the man over her, still holding both her hands in his larger ones, forcing her to stare into familiar features. His tanned face was scarred, but even still, she had to admit his resemblance to Desmon was undeniable.

Too tired for the moment, she lay there panting, using the break to catch her breath She knew it was a break the Goodwins likely wouldn't have given her. Just like a Goodwin wouldn't have simply blocked all her hits instead of fighting back.

She learned that the hard way.

The man showed her his right biceps, where a black inked wolf decorated his arm, underneath it was the name *Nightwind*, branding him as one of Desmon's pack.

He arched an eyebrow when she sucked in another hard breath. "Are you hearing me now? I'm Miles, Desmon's cousin. We haven't met yet, because I don't do social bullshit, but we're allies, okay? You can stop trying to rip my balls off now."

Amber was still panting, trying to catch her breath, but she gave a small nod and it must've been enough. He fell exhausted onto the bank next to her, lying there in wet clothes while his muscular chest rose and fell with sharp, hard breathes.

She touched her shoulder that ached, looked back in the direction they'd came from, and started crawling up the bank.

"Amber, please stop. I know you want to save your mate, but he's okay, and we have bigger problems," Miles whispered. "Desmon grew up fighting in these woods. I wouldn't have left him if I thought he couldn't handle himself. He's head alpha for a reason."

She shook her head frantically, refusing to give up on him. "He's hurt, I saw him, and—"

"*You're* hurt." He spoke in a soft growl, but the tone demanded she listen. "Look at yourself."

For the first time, Amber glanced down at her body, seeing the blood, various scrapes and bruises spread over her pale skin. It all looked as bad as it felt, because lying down let her feel absolutely everything. Her muscles were still seizing from whatever the blood did to her. Her shoulder was on fire from where Gary bit her. She noticed she was naked, too, really feeling the reality of it for the first time, and she put a hand over her breasts on instinct.

"I don't have any clothes," she whispered, feeling a rush of shame beneath the fear and pain. "I tore them off, and—"

"I have clothes for you." Miles sat up and pulled out a compact plastic bag of clothes from an inside pocket of his vest. "I had your sisters pack you something comfortable and easy to get out of before we left. I didn't tell Desmon, but I knew you'd probably need it. We don't change that many humans in Nightwind, but I used to work in the field. I know it's hard for new shifters to hold their forms, especially if they're changed under stressful circumstances."

"Thank you." Amber took the bag gratefully and pulled out one of her old concert shirts, loose fitting and comfortable. She tugged the black cotton material over her head, but didn't bother with the rest. Instead, she just forced the shirt over her knees, tenting it and hiding as she looked toward the clearing once more. "I have to go back."

"Listen to me, Amber, you're injured. Your body is under an enormous amount of stress right now, and we're in the middle Goodwin pack lands. The worst part is, your scent—"

Amber turned her head, hearing something far away in the clearing, from the direction where they'd left Desmon.

She took off.

From behind her, Miles muttered, "Are you fucking kidding me?" but she didn't let it stop her.

She didn't let the shirt stop her either, she ran with it on, her heartbeat thumping harder and louder in her ears. The smell was everywhere now, warm, spicy, safe. She needed it more than she had ever wanted anything for herself—ever—and she ran toward it with everything in her.

She heard Desmon before she saw him, his breathing mirroring her wild, panting desperation through the breeze in the leaves. He blended into the woods so beautifully in wolf form. Even with her brighter vision, the first thing she spotted of Desmon were his eyes glinting in the darkness. He was there. He was healthy, and she was so elated she could barely contain herself. Amber's trust for him was blind, unyielding, powerful enough for her jump at him, knowing he'd catch her.

Desmon changed that quickly, between one breath and the next, his big, strong arms tightening around her, cradling her smaller furry body against his smooth chest. Her shirt was wrapped around her like a blanket, trapping her paws, but she didn't care as he cuddled her tightly against him, keeping her there like he planned on never letting her go—which worked just fine for her, too.

"I got you." He hugged her tighter and kissed the top of her head, still walking with her as his entire body shook. "You're safe. You're strong. You're going to be okay, Angel."

She wanted to ask him if he was okay, too, and to be sure that Gary was dead and wasn't coming back. Worse, how many more of his pack were still out in the woods waiting for them? But she couldn't figure out how to shift again, and on a deeper level, it didn't matter too much. Amber knew she was safe. The proof was holding her and walking through the woods. That powerful, steady hum of life still vibrated off him stronger than ever, and like Desmon probably knew *she* was going to be okay, despite evidence to the contrary, Amber knew Desmon was just fine.

It was going to take a lot more than Gary Goodwin to take him down.

That was the last clear thought she had before the blur of trees and leaves faded out to nothing but a deep, fathomless starry blackness...and Amber passed out.

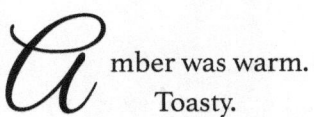mber was warm.
       Toasty.

The crackle of a fire drifted in and out of dreams that felt nice, even if she didn't really remember them, like Christmas mornings and sunshine in late afternoons all mixed up into one. Even better, the air around her smelled like men's cologne, only more natural. The best possible version of man, as if the earth made it just for her. She moaned and rolled over, sliding her hand over hard, sinewy muscle in appreciation.

"Ams." A hand brushed the fine hairs at her temple, tucking stray strands behind her ear. "Hey."

Amber blinked, seeing the fire first, orange and blue flames slowly coming into sharper focus as they danced hypnotically in the night. Desmon kept stroking her forehead, the curve of her neck, always touching her, like he needed the connection as much as she did.

She stretched then, feeling remarkably good. Her skin smelled really clean, like the river and soap rather than blood and dirt, as it had when she'd passed out, and Amber realized Desmon must've washed the Goodwins territory from her skin while she slept.

When she rolled over, Amber found herself on her back above a blanket laid over hard ground, with her head resting on Desmon's bare thigh. Her muscles felt so strong but relaxed somehow. Fluid and dependable. It was a strange feeling, as if she simply didn't have anything else to worry about where her body was concerned.

Absently, she felt her shoulder, remembering the crippling bite from Gary Goodwin. What she considered an ache in her shoulder while she was trying to get to Desmon, was actually something she realized now would have sent her to the hospital for a long time if she'd been human. A lot of things should have done her in, not just physically, but mentally as well. Strangely, it all felt quite recoverable, but it shouldn't be—should it?

Her hair was braided, something she hadn't done since she was young, and again, she knew Desmon must've done it, but it didn't bother her.

"How are you?" Desmon sounded scared to ask.

She looked up at him then and took another mental stock of her injures, before she admitted, "I feel great, like a million bucks. You'd never know anything bad happened. It's a really weird sensation, feeling this strong and healthy. It's like waking up as a superhero."

"I'm sure bloodlust is helping that along." Desmon sighed, looking conflicted. "And you've been asleep since last night, so..."

"So?" she pressed when he hesitated, realizing it was dark again outside.

She'd been passed out for almost twenty-four hours.

"That's how shifters heal," he explained simply. "Sleep."

"That makes sense." She thought of six-year-old Desmon, relying on her to hide him while he slept so he could heal from being hit by a car. She glanced around their new hideout, finding that it was a cave of some sort, vast and echoing with a cold wind that came in from the back. "What is this place?"

"We're on the edge of Nightwind land, up in the mountains on the south end. It's isolated out here. We use it to train teenage pups in survival a couple times a year."

"Where's your cousin?" she asked curiously.

"Out playing survival. He's watching the area for me."

"That's nice of him," Amber whispered. "I feel bad."

"Don't. It's his favorite game. He'd stay up here playing it all the time if I didn't make him live down with the pack. Miles is a lone wolf. He doesn't crave companionship like the rest of us do. It happens sometimes. Even before his accident, he never wanted the responsibility of pack life. He worked for the Alliance and traveled."

Amber caressed his leg. "I like Miles."

"I'm glad." Desmon smiled when he said it. "He's the only blood family I have left out here."

"Have you talked to my sisters?"

"They know you're with me," Desmon assured her. "They're staying with Jason and Brandi while we're gone. I want them on pack land right now. Jason agreed to follow Bea to school and back, since things are obviously tense with the Goodwins. Jazz gave Katie a job in the office. He's paying her double, so she'd quit the other one. They'll be fine."

"And your pack?"

"Jazz is taking care of them." Desmon picked up a stick from a pile next to him and threw it on the fire. "You don't want to talk about you? We're going to discuss everyone else instead?"

"Sure." She smiled up at him, because his hair hung long and loose over his tanned shoulders. She tilted her head, seeing that he was completely bare under the firelight, the flames reflecting off his smooth, tan skin. Amber felt the same warmth spread deeper insider her, flooding into her fingers and toes in an intoxicating rush. "You're naked."

"That happens to shifters sometimes," he agreed with a shrug. "Out in the mountains, shifting back and forth, clothes are just—"

"A massive pain in the ass," she finished for him. "I get it now."

She smelled the shirt she was wearing, so different from her concert one. The simple red cotton was pure Desmon, and she inhaled deeply, savoring it. "Mmm, this must be yours."

"It is." Desmon seemed embarrassed as he admitted, "I did it on purpose. I wanted my scent on you."

"That's okay. I'll never complain about that. You smell delicious."

"You too." He closed his eyes as he said it. "Big time."

"How strong is it?" she asked, a sliver of fear making its way past the warm, safe feeling of waking up next to Desmon.

"Enough to have to hide you way up in the mountains until the scent of you being in heat fades?" Desmon flinched as he said it. "Depending on what happens, we could be up here for a few more days."

"And do you like it?" Amber's voice was husky, compelling even to her own ears. "As much as I like smelling you?"

"I'm sure I like your scent a lot more than you like mine." Desmon seemed confident about it. "Especially after being in this cave with you all day."

"I don't know about that." She pulled the edge of the shirt she was wearing over her face, breathing him in. "You smell pretty damn good."

Desmon chuckled, sounding a little pained, but still genuinely amused. "I like your wolf, Angel. Seeing her is nice, even if the circumstances are awful."

"Is it a separate thing? This wolf you talk about?" Amber fingered the braid in her hair, feeling anxious with all the energy pulsing through her body. Half of her wanted to get up and run a marathon, the other part was perfectly happy lying with her head in Desmon's lap. "Do I get a multiple-personality issue to go along with my superhero powers?"

"It's just a different mindset, and somewhere along the way our people labeled it as separate. It's not really. Most of the time we do it to excuse bad behavior, but sometimes it's just adorable as hell. Female wolves, anyway. Male wolves, not so much."

"Tell me about male wolves then," Amber asked with a teasing smile, smelling his shirt once more. "Are they so bad?"

"Annoying on good days, territorial and dangerous on most, deadly for a few," Desmon explained simply. "If they didn't have adorable, smart, cunning females to hold them up, they'd be fucking useless to the planet."

There was a growl of fury in his voice, and she had to ask, "Did you kill him?"

"Yeah." Desmon threw more sticks on the fire. "He's dead."

"Are you in trouble for it?" Amber asked fearfully, because she wasn't sure about shifter laws. "I mean, is it murder in your world?"

"It's your world now too, and yes, it could be if the powers that be decide to look at it that way. I killed him on Goodwin pack land, and I'm not allowed to be there. We are not allies with the Goodwins. We're not even in negotiations, and the Alliance is very serious about territories. Leroy already reported me. Jazz just called and said an Alliance Enforcer is coming out in the next day or so." Desmon held up the phone next to him, looking disgusted by it as he sat there naked in the cave. "That's probably what woke you up."

"So, you're in trouble?"

Desmon nodded once more. "A little bit."

"And it's my fault."

"It's not your fault. It's not mine, either. The Goodwins did this." Desmon snarled the words, sounding like he believed them down to his core. "You're my mate, and he was attacking you. I'm allowed to protect you. If they want to put me on trial for that, I'll proudly do it. I feel no shame for what I did. It's my honor to protect you. Nature gave me that right. Fuck the Alliance if they don't like it."

Desmon leaned over her, resting his forehead in the soft place between her breasts. Amber threaded her fingers through his long, silky black hair, holding him against her.

It was so much quieter in the mountains, with just the crackle of the fire in the night and the sounds of the breeze from outside the cave.

"I see why Miles likes it up here. It's peaceful," she whispered softly. "And it smells so good."

Desmon let out a pained laughed, still bent over her. "I don't think it's the cave you're smelling, unless you love the scent of bat shit."

"No, it's like Christmas cookies." She went from caressing his hair to trailing her fingers down his bare back. "Spiced molasses with extra cinnamon."

"Please do *not* tell anyone you think I smell like cookies." Desmon kissed her neck as he said it, "I *would* let you take a bite if you wanted to, though."

Amber used her hold on his hair and lifted his head at the sound in his voice, forcing him to meet her gaze. She saw that Desmon's pupils had dilated, his light eyes vibrant in the darkness, making him look powerful and primal under the flames.

"You want me to bite you?" she asked, feeling all that untapped energy start to morph into something decadent and hungry.

"I do, very much." Desmon's voice vibrated with the growl of his animal. "You've tasted *him*. Not me. It's a stupid territorial thing with males. I love you. It doesn't matter. But it's been a really long couple of days and—"

He stopped with a choked snarl of shock when Amber suddenly bit into his wrist.

"Oh fuck."

Desmon growled then, and Amber's entire body seemed to vibrate with the sound as his heady taste filled her senses. It was a thousand times better than cookies, and Amber whimpered when Desmon pulled his wrist away, but then moaned when he captured her mouth with his in a hard kiss. His tongue pushed in deep, their lips sticky with his blood, but it didn't matter.

His taste made everything better according to Amber.

The wave of desire was blinding, wiping out all rational thought as she crawled over him, and straddled Desmon on the cave floor. They kissed open-mouthed, hungry, with his hard cock rubbing against the thin cotton panties she wore under Desmon's shirt.

Why had Desmon even bothered?

"Get 'em off," she panted against his lips, even as she sat on him, wrapping her thighs around his hips. "Please."

Desmon held Amber as he got to his knees on the blanket and lay her out on it. Then he was over her, his weight deliciously heavy as he kissed and licked the sensitive skin of her neck. Amber pushed him away only to pull off the shirt she was wearing. Desmon tugged the panties down her thighs at the same time, and Amber dimly noticed the sound of ripping material until they were both blissfully bare.

His teeth were long, sharp against her nipple, but he didn't bite. He sucked instead, making her writhe beneath him as he moved over to the other one. The tease only caused the bliss burn brighter. Sweat ran down from her temples, her skin grew dewy with the heat of the fire and it only added to the dazed need.

Amber's fingers were tight in his hair by the time he abandoned her breasts and moved lower. He nipped at her hip but didn't break the skin and she knew Desmon was holding back.

"You can bite me," she gasped, frantic with passion. "You don't have to be gentle, you can-"

She sucked in a sharp breath when he pushed her legs apart and slid his thumb between the folds of her pussy. She was dripping wet, and Desmon growled as he pushed one thick finger inside like he couldn't resist, and then another, until he was fucking her with his hand. Amber tightened her hold on his hair, her hips arching into the stroke of his fingers over and over again.

He nipped at the inside of her thigh in warning, forcing her legs open wider for him with a rough slide of his hand. She still jerked from the shock of indulgence when Desmon licked the full length of her pussy and sucked on her clit.

It was the way he did it, so ravenous.

Amber went wild.

She kept trying to get closer somehow, to find relief, and Desmon was forced to hold her hip with his free hand, pinning her down while she fought for a release. The warmth of his mouth, the feel of his tongue against her, the stroke of his fingers still inside her. It was almost too much, the stimulation, a white-wash of extasy no human could survive when Desmon left her nowhere to hide. The pleasure was suddenly everywhere, leaving her gasping and crying out under the storm.

Once her climax broke free, it took a long time for the extasy to wane, reducing Amber to breathless growls that were more wolf than human.

Desmon was shaking as he crawled back over her. His scent was everywhere, throbbing off his taut body, drowning out all but him. She could feel hair then skin on his shoulders and arms, meaning he was shifting back and forth somehow, but it didn't bother Amber at all. She loved him completely, in a way she never truly understood until she thought she'd lost him in the forest.

"In me." She didn't recognize the low, husky rasp of her voice, but it didn't matter. "Please."

"Amber, listen, no," Desmon was panting, but he still managed to pull back despite Amber wrapping her arms around him. His voice was more wolf than human as he explained, "I had to wash Leroy Goodwin's blood off your naked body and I've been smelling you all day in bloodlust. I'll mate you if I take you, and everything else has been without your permission. We can't unless you want it, because it's forever for both of us. You're a shifter, too. We don't get to walk away like humans do. I can take care of you without it, and—"

"It's okay." She pulled him back down, forcing his head into the curve of her neck, and Desmon went willingly, still shaking in her arms. "I want it—all of it."

"You can't be sure of that. You're suffering from bloodlust and you were changed against your will," Desmon argued, but it lost some of its fierceness when Amber wrapped her legs around his waist. "I'm strong, but I'm not *this* strong, Angel."

"That's okay. You don't have to be strong all the time," she promised him, her sharp nails in his shoulders. "I want to be your mate."

It must've been good enough, because Desmon reached down, grabbing her thigh, holding her open as he looked between them, watching himself take her when he shifted his hips to slide in.

"Des," Amber moaned, throwing her head back at the feel of his thick cock stretching her. The ripple of pleasure was sheer sin, so rich and multilayered she could only open wider to the thrust, arching her hips to take more of him. "Oh Jesus!"

Desmon responded by pulling out and pushing in harder, making Amber cry out. Then he did it again, still holding himself up on one arm to watch the slide of his cock deep into her pussy. Amber pulled him down on top of her, desperate to be skin to skin.

She needed to feel his weight.

His strength and power.

Desmon gave her what she wanted, letting her overwhelm herself with him, holding Amber to him tightly when he thrust deeper. He started fucking her fast.

Savage.

Amber met him stroke for stroke. Her nails became sharp and cruel, drawing blood. Her teeth grew long, and she bit hard, letting the taste, smell and feel of him wash away the nightmare.

Her climax hit even more violently the second time, and she clung to him when her entire body shook from the force of it. She pulled Desmon down with her, a part of Amber knowing he was partially shifted when he bit into the soft spot at the curve of her neck, making another violent surge of pleasure crash through her.

She bit him harder, sharp teeth sinking into the soft skin, letting all that warm male strength sink into her veins, tying them together forever. Amber didn't understand the exact details of how he bound them together, but she still knew instinctively that they were, and she was fine with it.

A part of her was ecstatic even, like she'd been running a lifelong race to get to this exact moment. She understood why they called the wolf separate, simply because her primal side was so completely unburdened by the other mundane worries of humanity. Things were much easier when it was just survival, but Desmon was still shaky long after he'd pulled out of her.

The freedom wasn't a novelty to him, and she suspected he was more man than wolf by the time the two of them settled into peaceful quiet in front of the fire. For a long time, she held him rather than ask why, letting his head rest in the soft place between her bare breasts.

"Des." She caressed his silky hair and asked, "Did you braid my hair?"

"Was that wrong?" he asked quickly. "I wasn't sure if you'd have a problem with it or not, but you had their scent all over you, and your hair was tangled and dirty, so I—"

"It's fine," she assured him. "We're mates, right?"

Desmon nodded. "We're mates."

"Officially?"

"Yes." His voice was a rasp of uncertainty. "You know I would've done it differently if I had a choice. This wasn't how it was supposed to happen for you—in a cave."

"Did Miles tell you how I reacted when I'd thought you'd died?" Her voice cracked when she said it. The pain burst open, the memory nearly stealing her breath. "I went crazy. I wanted to die with you. I tried everything to jump in that fight. It wasn't brave, it was cowardly. I don't want to do this alone anymore. I need you with me."

"I need you, too, so much," he whispered like he truly understood. "And you're stuck with me now. But I'm worried about this Gary problem. There's a small chance, if it goes to trial, they could—"

Amber covered his lips with her fingers. "Not now."

Desmon looked up at her, his gaze still wolf-like and dilated, but he nodded in agreement. "I'm also not sure how well your human birth control will work now that you're a shifter, but there are ways for our females to prevent pregnancy."

"Why?" she asked. "Do want to avoid children?"

"No!" The word burst out of Desmon quickly with the snarl of his primal side, like it was something bone deep. "I want pups. I want them to inherit this pack and have a safe place to raise their families. It's important to me, but I would give it up if you didn't want it, too."

"I want them," she assured him. "I've always wanted children. You remember I told you it was my ex who was against them, not me. I've been feeling my clock ticking for a while. I guess that's not a problem anymore."

Desmon smiled at that. "Nope."

Amber reached up, pulling at the delicate skin at the corners of her eyes. "Was it like an instant facelift? I haven't looked in a mirror yet. Do I look twenty-one again?"

"I don't know." He laughed, but the sound seemed foreign, like he'd walked through fire to get there as he studied her face. "You look the same to me. Perfect."

"I smell better though."

"Oh, fuck yes, you do," he assured her with another smile.

Then he rolled over and sucked on one of her nipples, making her gasp when the pleasure washed over like it had never waned to begin with

Forgetting everything else ended up being easy for both of them —at least for a little while.

17

TWO DAYS LATER

*D*esmon heard Miles let himself into the house, and Jazz shortly thereafter. He knew they came with news and were politely waiting for him to come down, rather than bother Amber while she was still recovering.

He wanted to stay in the cave longer, but they had been forced to return because of the investigation. The Alliance Enforcer had showed up at Desmon's house last night and interviewed all of them for a long time before he headed over to talk to the Goodwins.

Miles knew this particular Alliance Enforcer. The two of them used to serve together, but Desmon was still incredibly nervous.

He took his time slipping out from underneath Amber, pulled his jeans on as silently as possible, and closed the bedroom door gently. Then he went down the stairs when he was sure Amber wouldn't be disturbed

He entered the kitchen, finding his cousin sitting at the table. Miles was drinking a fresh cup of coffee. Jazz was pouring himself a new one, but they both had the look of wolves who had stopped talking the second Desmon opened the door upstairs.

"Morning," Jazz said casually. "How's Amber feeling?"

"She's fine." Desmon tried to stay civil, but he was still way too on edge for pleasantries. "What happened with the Alliance?"

Miles set his cup on the table and lowered his gaze, making it obvious he didn't come with news he was happy to share. "The thing is, Des—"

"He's getting away with some sort of fine after what he did to her, despite knowing she was mine?" Desmon's voice was completely inhuman. "That better be the bad news, because if I have to go to trial for saving my mate—"

Miles looked up at Desmon and flinched. "No trial, but no fine for the Goodwins, either."

Desmon stared in disbelief. "What?"

"It was Leroy's blood that made her wolf, and you trespassed on Goodwin land to steal her before he had a chance with her. Not to mention the shit-show at the border." Miles almost sounded like he agreed with the Alliance. "Trust me on this, Des. Let it go."

Desmon stared at his cousin like he didn't know him. "Are you actually okay with this? You think it's fair that he's getting away with stealing my mate?"

"Seriously?" Miles growled, clearly insulted. "You're asking me that?"

"Well, they're *your* buddies!"

"I grew up fighting on the same borders you did. I know who the Goodwins are, but Carl's hands were tried. He did the best he could for us, and it was a lot!" Miles barked, like he believed it "You know Leroy, he manipulated the facts. No one ever said he was stupid. On paper, he has the better case. Ask Jazz—"

"Leave me out of it." Jazz held up his hands, his voice growly, too. "I still can't believe this is happening. The Goodwins come off looking like they're human advocates now. That's bullshit."

"*You* can't believe it? I feel like I woke up on a different fucking planet," Desmon agreed with Jazz, before turning back to Miles. "Look, I'm sorry. I know none of this is your fault. You had my back. Amber and I appreciate it more than you will ever know, but it's obvious they lied their asses off! Gary saw her in town! He was sniffing after her! Did you remind him of that?"

"It doesn't prove anything, Des. With the Alliance, it's all about concrete proof, and Gary wasn't even there when she was turned. So, like it or not, none of it means anything. They can't start putting shifters on trial without evidence. You don't want that. No one does. Even if this sucks right now, they're good rules." Miles sounded miserable. "Leroy said Amber sideswiped one of his teenage pups with a car. When she got out to check on him, she tripped in the mud and hit her head. He said the other one, Rich, is full grown, but he has more wolf than human for smarts. He thought she was dying and wanted to save the pretty human. Rich gave her some blood and threw her in the trunk rather than let her die on the road."

"Humans have emergency services. He had a phone," Desmon argued. "He could've called 9-1-1 and left, instead he hogtied her with bungie cords!"

"They inspected her car, Des. It was obvious she hit something," Jazz sighed.

"Because they set her up! That's human hunting, and last I checked, it's still illegal as hell."

"Yeah, but Carl interviewed Rich, and he kind of agreed with Leroy about the guy. He thinks it's a miracle Rich didn't just eat her when he thought she was dying, especially on the full moon. You know the Alliance has to make certain allowances for rural packs. They think we run wild too much out here."

"Well." Jazz tilted his head and took a sip of his coffee. "They're not wrong about that."

"Nope." Miles sighed again. "Anyway, Rich and the pup came off as saints taking her back to Leroy, who changed Amber right away when he saw they accidently used too much blood trying to heal her. Then he called us to make sure we knew she was one of his now. He planned to celebrate the full moon with his new pack bitch...until *you* showed up. If you hadn't mated her, we could've had to give Amber back to him. Also, you avoided being executed. No trial. You're free and clear, which was all I cared about at this point."

Desmon still couldn't let it go. "What about the conflict at the border? That attack was preplanned."

"We're guilty of it, too." Miles shrugged. "Jazz and Jason ran our enforcers across the north border on purpose. They showed up to the fight as a diversion for us, and the Goodwins lost four wolves in that fight on top of Gary. We didn't lose anyone. That doesn't exactly make us look like the victimized pack on paper *or* during a trial."

"And what about the fact that Amber didn't want him? She already knew she was my mate when they changed her. That doesn't matter? Anyone can just grab a shifter's mate and shove her in the trunk? The Alliance is good with that? My mate's pain is being ignored because I train my wolves to fight better than Leroy's do?"

"Again, there's no proof. You saw what Amber was like in the woods. Lots of weres get changed under stressful conditions, but we don't want the Alliance to start putting a ban on making new shifters. It's one of those bullshit loopholes they can't fix, but they can't alter it either, because the changeover is confusing. It's scary for new shifters. They're not thinking clearly. They don't know how to hold form or process new information. It's not fair, but it's still not dependable evidence to put a shifter to death over. They'd listen to her statement, but in a trial, her testimony wouldn't count."

Desmon snorted. "That's convenient."

Miles winced again. "So, Carl did me a huge favor, chalked it up in the report to full moon wolf shenanigans, and walked away. The fact that you were fucking her before she was taken made him especially sympathetic. She's your mate. He understands why you went after her, even if his hands are tied by bureaucratic bullshit. He said he'd fix her were registration with the Alliance and update the Nightwind files about your mating. He did the best he could under the circumstance."

"Is full moon wolf shenanigans a genuine thing they list on Alliance reports?" Jazz asked curiously.

"Yeah." Miles let out a bitter laugh. "They just fucking give up on wolves for the full moon. We killed five shifters and got away with it. What does that tell you?"

Out of the blue, Desmon lost control of his wolf, which was still feeling more than a little under attack where Amber was concerned. He reached forward, grabbed the edge of the table and flipped it over, sending dishes to the floor and napkins flying.

Jazz jumped back, but Miles just growled in annoyance. "Fuck me, Des, are you a pup now? You can't fucking control it?"

"You're going to make me tell my mate he's getting off free and clear?" Desmon roared at both of them. "I have to go up there and tell her shifters don't give a shit about what happened to her?"

"There's a reason full moon wolf shenanigans is the most written complaint. Pack wolves *are* wild. Look at this, and you're the one in charge!" Miles ran both hands over his face and took a deep breath like he was trying to get ahold of his own beast. "Des, I love you, but —Goddamn, you and Amber are well suited, 'cause your alpha side can make you a legitimate motherfucker sometimes."

"Now you're making me the bad guy?" Desmon's voice cracked with hurt, the pain crushing in on him without warning. "I'm the big bad wolf."

A ghost of a smile showed on Miles's scarred face. "You say that like it's a bad thing."

Desmon growled and walked out of the kitchen. "I'm going back to bed with my mate."

He felt the sting in his eyes, realizing he was fighting off actual tears of frustration and anger. What the hell was he going to tell Amber? He could barely face her, but he couldn't stay away either.

Miles caught him before he could get to the stairs, because the asshole was too fucking fast in human form. No shifter should spend that much time sulking around in skin. Desmon tried to break out of his cousin's hold when he wrapped his arms around him, hugging him tightly from behind like his father used to do when he was little and Desmon couldn't control his temper. Only, Desmon wasn't little anymore and he didn't want to be reminded of his father. Not right now.

To humans, it would probably look like a fight.

To wolves, it was more playful than anything. Even if Desmon didn't see it like that while he was rolling on the carpet, trying to break away, he knew Miles did, which only served to piss him off more.

"This is all well and good if you need an outlet before you go upstairs to your mate, but you know this isn't Miles's fault," Jazz whispered after a few long minutes of Miles doing most of the wrestling and Desmon doing most of the growling and losing. "They found Gary's body three miles inland, on the opposite side of our border. You killed him on his own land, and you admitted to it."

"I don't give a shit! I'm trying to make her like us!" Desmon roared when the anger at his cousin morphed into full-fledged fear of losing his mate. He couldn't stop seeing Amber naked under Gary Goodwin in the woods. All her pain. All her humiliation. It felt like his fault. "I want her to feel safe!"

"Good luck with that, because it's a lie. No one's safe. No one on this whole fucking planet. It's dangerous to be human. It's dangerous to be wolf, too." Miles let Desmon go to stare down at his own scarred arm pointedly, before he glanced back to him. "*Living* is dangerous. We're all going to die one day, and maybe having a mate now makes it harder. I wouldn't know. But you're going to have to learn how to deal with it."

Desmon rolled onto his back when Miles let him go. He looked up at the ceiling of the house built for his family by the pack, trying desperately to calm himself down before he went back to Amber. His mother was content now. She and Hope loved the Hunter pack, and Arizona, but she had suffered so much being a shifter and it haunted him as much as Amber's pain did.

"Do you think she would've been happier if he never changed her?" Desmon asked both of them. "What if he never found her? And she lived out her life not knowing there was a wolf who was born to adore her?"

"Who?" Jazz asked him, sounding mystified.

"My mother."

"Okay, no." Miles rolled over on the carpet next to him and threaded his fingers behind his head. "No wonder your wolf has you flipping over tables. You can't let your mind go there, Des. Amber's not going to end up like your mother."

Desmon shook his head. "You don't know that. Like you said, living is dangerous. Anything could happen to me, and then what? Either she dies with me, or she's stuck alone with shifter pups."

"I wouldn't let that happen. I wouldn't leave your mate and pups unprotected." Miles gestured at Jazz standing over them. "And he won't let it happen either." He pointed to the front door next. "None of them are going to let that happen to her. Your enforcers support you. All your wolves do. We have a solid pack now. Break all the tables you want, but you know it wasn't the same back then after my parents died. That was Uncle Nesso's mistake, letting Albert stay, leaning on an alpha he knew he couldn't trust."

"It already happened. Look at what they did to her," Desmon whispered miserably. "Fucking Goodwins, they'll always be plotting, always trying for this land. It's been generations of this shit now. My pups are going to be stuck dealing with them one day."

"Fuck that, no. We're going to get the Goodwins." Jazz sat down on the carpet next to Desmon, looking fierce. "I'm not playing this time. I'm done with those motherfuckers. We're taking them down after this. Leroy wants to start shit with us? He likes to play around and fuck with us every full moon? Fine, let's finish it for him this time."

Miles rolled over and propped his head in his hand. "I'm game."

"You're always game," Desmon huffed, because Miles would show up at the gates of hell if a fight was supposed to be there. "And who'll protect the rest of Nightwind when all of us are in deep with the Alliance for ripping apart the Goodwins?"

"Yeah, 'cause we're great at following rules and keeping our noses clean." Miles let out a snort of disbelief. "This situation with Amber was an isolated fuck up, but it's not our standard. Look at what we did to that pack who tried to get Brandi from Jason. If we cleaned that up—"

"Those were untrained, unseasoned city wolves pretending they were a real pack," Desmon reminded him. "The Goodwins are not city wolves. Leroy knows what he's doing, and even if he hadn't manipulated the Alliance, the Goodwins know this land almost as well as we do."

"Yeah, almost, but their tracking only takes them so far," Miles reminded him. "And we'll get better. I'll teach a scenting class for the older cubs. You were right about that. We'll do more survival training. Males and females. They won't like it, but it'll be good for them."

"We'll do it with all of them," Jazz jumped in, sounding determined. "I'll take groups of the enforcers up into the mountains a few times a week for extra training. We'll start sleeping outside more, and toughen them up too. I don't have a mate, what the hell do I have to do."

Desmon considered them for a moment. "It would be nice to have actual peace in this area. To give Amber the pups she wants without worrying every day about war stealing them from her."

"And all those poor females in Goodwin." Jazz's voice was distant. "We should do this. Not just for Amber, but for Marcy too."

Desmon sat up and rested his hand on his knee as the idea took root. That wild and crazy dream he barely dared entertain of raising his pups with Amber on land he wasn't constantly fighting to protect. Free and clear territory, no border wars, like the Hunter Pack in Arizona where females went to feel safe and protected.

"Sucks I'm on the Alliance's shit list now," Desmon whispered, knowing the report was going to be filed, even if he hadn't been tried or fined. "That'll make it a lot harder."

"If only you knew someone with inside knowledge of all the ins and outs of the Alliance," Miles mused thoughtfully. "Packs change hands, Des. Territories expand. Gary's gone. Leroy lost his back up, and you know that hurts. Old alphas disappear, new ones take over. There's a lot of females over in Goodwin who wouldn't complain if they got you for an alpha instead of Leroy. It won't be easy, but it can be done."

"It'll still take a long time, years maybe. I can't risk going on trial and getting executed by the Alliance. I have a mate now. We have to be really careful. I could doom Amber with me, especially if we don't have pups for her to stay alive for."

"You know we made mistakes. You left Gary behind." Jazz gave Desmon a knowing look. "You can't do that next time. No body. No proof, and the Alliance looks the other way. That was crazy dangerous."

Miles winced, like that was something he was avoiding bringing up because he'd been surprised by it too. Desmon hadn't been willing to risk his mate seeing anything more traumatizing. He hadn't told Miles the truth until they crossed the border.

"Okay, I fucked up. I should've eaten him. If Amber wasn't there, I would've," Desmon growled, then turned when he felt the back of his neck prickling in warning—only to see Amber standing at the stop of the stairs. "And that's perfect."

Somehow he hadn't heard her or smelled her coming, which didn't help Desmon's overall state of mind.

"I heard the yelling." Amber wore one of his t-shirts that hung down to her knees, and folded her arms, exposing her bare thighs.

"I have to take off." Miles rolled back and jumped to his feet when Amber started walking down the stairs. "Hey, Amber. I'll catch you later."

"You don't have to leave," she argued as Miles walked for the door.

"Yeah, I do." Miles turned the knob without a backwards glance. "We'll do dinner sometime. My place. It's quiet there. You'll like it."

She stopped at the foot of the stairs, looking at Desmon and Jazz still sprawled out on the carpet after Miles left.

"I guess it didn't go well with the Shifter Alliance."

Desmon shook his head, feeling too sick to do more than that.

"They're not going to do anything to the Goodwins," Jazz explained for him. "It was lucky, but Desmon needs a little time to see that."

"I see it," Desmon whispered next to him, before he looked back to Amber. "I just wanted better news for you, Angel."

Amber tilted her head, and stared at the destroyed table in the kitchen, her expression making her appear distant. "Would you really have eaten him if I hadn't been there?"

Desmon looked to her as the back of his neck got hot. He made slow work of getting to his feet rather than answer her.

"Forget Des. *I* would've eaten him if I'd known it was going to cost us this much headache," Jazz deadpanned and took another drink of his coffee that he had casually brought with him from the kitchen while Miles and Desmon fought. "In fact, I would've done it without the headache. I would've done it just because the Goodwins are a fucking pain in our ass."

"Jazz—" Desmon felt his lip twitch in spite of everything.

"I don't even understand what the debate is. Look at what he did to her." Jazz growled, suddenly looking vicious. "He's a fucking human hunter. I'd eat him twice—with barbeque sauce."

"Bye, Jazz." Desmon gave him a sharp look. "Only call if it's an emergency. It's still our mating honeymoon, and we've been through a lot. Obviously, my wolf needs more time to calm down. Tell the others."

Jazz held up his phone as he stood. "Already ahead of you."

Desmon avoided looking at Amber as Jazz showed himself out. He was embarrassed over losing his temper so soon after mating her, but his wolf was still feral and reckless over what had happened to Amber. There was guilt too, because she had no choice about this being her life. He didn't want her to hate being a shifter, but they weren't getting off to a very good start.

"Don't panic. It's a weird, sensitive subject with Jazz. The pack buried his father, and he's still pissed off about it. Marcy never got a grave. It's unfair," Desmon explained after Jazz left. "We do bury our dead to honor them like humans do—most of the time."

"But you also eat them," Amber clarified softly. "The other alpha, Leroy, he talked about eating their prey, and he didn't mean rabbits."

"If they're human hunting, then yes, I'm sure they're eating them. It'd be dangerous to risk human remains being found, just like it was dangerous to risk Gary being found," Desmon explained, hoping it was enough, but knowing it wasn't. "Truth is, wolves will eat just about anything in the name of survival. We're not picky eaters."

"You hunt animals for meat—and you hunt people for the same reason. It's a problem."

"Nightwind doesn't do that," Desmon assured Amber when she wouldn't let it go. "We have *never* done that. Even when Albert was in charge. We didn't socialize with humans, but we didn't hunt them, either, I promise. My mother was human once, remember? My father had respect for them, enough to fall in love with one, and he instilled that in this pack. The Shifter Alliance has laws to prevent human hunting, but there are still a lot of immoral asshole shifters. Just like there's a lot of immoral humans, and it does happen, same as human crimes happen." He shrugged, trying to remind himself of that fact as much as Amber. "We're not perfect, and I know you wouldn't have chosen this life, but—"

"You're better than most of your kind," she finished for him. "You're an honorable wolf, and an even more honorable man."

It wasn't what he was going to say, but he went with it. "Okay."

"You try your best to keep your pack safe, even from themselves. You make rules to keep humans in this town safe, too." Amber gave him a soft smile. "The world is better with you in it, and I'm lucky to have you for a mate."

Desmon raised his eyebrows and smiled back in surprise. "If you say, so."

Amber walked up and wrapped her arms around him. Desmon took a shuddering breath at the rush of warmth that rushed down his spine. He hugged Amber back and kissed the top of her head, relieved beyond words that she didn't hate him or what she had been forced to become.

"I'm sorry about the trouble." Amber rested her cheek against his bare chest. "But I'm so glad you showed up when you did. I know you risked a lot, Des. Your freedom. Your position as alpha. Your whole pack."

"It doesn't matter." Desmon tightened his arms around her, and the anger fell out of him like it had never existed to begin with when he realized Amber was healthy and happy in his arms. "Really, you being safe is the only thing I care about. The rest is just noise."

"Can those Goodwins hurt me or my sisters now that they know who we are?"

"No, we're going to move your sisters onto pack land permanently, and I'll make sure the Goodwins know they're under my protection. As for you...you're my mate, and a pretty tough bitch, if I do say so myself. You'll be able to protect yourself." Desmon felt the pride swell in his chest, and an excitement for the future slowly started to grow. "I'm going to teach you how to fight, Angel. We'll do survival training, and sleep together outside. It'll be fun."

Amber tilted her head, giving him a calculating look. "Don't think I'm going to start hunting deer and rabbit with you, 'cause there's no way."

"Sure." Desmon smiled in spite of everything. "You'll be the first vegetarian wolf."

"You don't believe me?" Amber asked, sounding genuinely indignant.

"No, I don't." Desmon was pretty sure of it. "We're carnivores. It wouldn't be good for you, and it's my job to keep you healthy." He caressed her arm and leaned down to kiss the soft spot behind her ear. "I could teach you to wolf right now, if you want?"

"Why, are you in the mood to hunt?" Amber's voice was teasing.

"If that's what we're calling it." He breathed in the warm, spicy scent of her arousal, and leaned down to bury his face against the curve of her neck. His wolf was still reckless under the surface. He needed a lot more time with his mate to assure himself she was safe, to know she was alive and healthy and not leaving again. "I need to taste you, Angel."

Amber obviously needed it, too, and let her head fall to the side in submission. "Go ahead."

The need was blinding. He nearly howled with it as he started kissing and licking her neck, making her moan, and the rush went straight to his cock. He cupped Amber's bare ass. She wore nothing beneath his shirt, and Desmon knew she was losing the human fondness for modesty faster than she probably realized.

A part of him was sad for it. Her humanity was slipping away like a distant memory. It was as it should be, but he wanted to make it easier, to hide her from the death of it.

Desmon forced her tighter against him, letting her feel how much he wanted her. The way she melted into him with a low, soft growl made the fire burn brighter. He slipped his hand between her legs, savoring the smooth, slick feel of her pussy as he found her clit.

Her gasp, the way she gripped at his shoulder, it hit him hard then, the realization that she was his, and she wasn't a fragile human anymore. She was a powerful bitch. *His mate.* A partner to stand by him with their pack. It felt like a miracle, something he didn't dare dream about coming true for so long.

She lost something, but she gained something, too, as long as Desmon did his job as mate correctly. He would make sure she grew to love what she'd gained far more than she mourned what she'd lost.

Right now, she was here with him.

And they were bonded.

Amber was his forever.

Gratitude collided with the lust while he touched her, listening to the sounds she made as she got wetter and wetter. He wanted to bite her, to fuck her, and drown himself completely in the taste and feel of his mate—but he waited this time. A part of him had always been hungry for the soft comfort of fucking his mate just to connect with her.

He suspected the last of the bloodlust had left her during their time in the cave. Now it was just their chemistry as she tangled her fingers in his hair encouragingly. He enjoyed going slower, admiring the flush of her skin and the low growls that became more wolf-like than human the longer he touched her. He alternated between rubbing her clit and slipping his fingers in deep, fucking her with them, making Amber cling to him harder with low gasps for more.

"Now, Des!" Amber forced his face tighter against her neck this time, obviously fed up with his teasing. "Bite me. Fuck me." She was panting, desperate, flooding the room with the smell of her need. "What're you waiting for?"

"I'm being gentle." Desmon smiled playfully. "Don't you—" He growled when Amber bit him, hard, right in the tender curve of his neck. "Fuck!"

The rush was blinding and, like in the cave, it wiped out all sense of reason. He'd planned to take his time now that they were in his home instead of the woods, to watch her come for him, begging, breathless and sweaty while he touched her, but the joke was on him. The white-hot flood of lust had him pushing her against the sofa instead, the two of them falling against the cushions.

He tugged her head back and caught her mouth with his. Amber's lips were red with his blood, the taste of it still on her when she met his hunger with the same fiery ferocity, and it only fueled him more. They lay there kissing, open-mouthed, tongues bushing until they were both shaking.

Amber pulled the shirt over her head and tossed it to the ground, leaving her completely naked beneath him. Then, it was her hands pulling the button to his jeans open. Her sharp canine teeth biting his bottom lip, neck and shoulders, leaving them both sticky with blood and slick sweat as the need heated their skins. It was her nails raking down his bare back, and that's exactly how Desmon liked it.

He didn't bother to take his jeans off, instead he shoved them past his hips when Amber wrapped her legs around him. She fisted his hair, forcing his lips to hers once more and rubbed herself against the thick length of his dick—over and over again—teasing him with the slick feel of her pussy.

Unable to wait, Desmon grabbed her hips, holding her down as he pushed in.

"God!" Amber cried out, and bowed into the thrust of his cock, letting Desmon drown in the warm, wet feel of her wrapped around him.

Mindless with the need now, Desmon hooked his arms under both her legs, opening her wide to take him when he started fucking her hard. Their growls and moans blended between harsh kisses and passionate bites. Amber arched into him, dropping her head back, letting him suck her tits, and Desmon couldn't resist catching her tight pink nipples between his teeth in a way he would've never done with a human.

This was were sex, intense and ferocious, and like before, Amber surrendered herself to it completely. Desmon had no idea how long it would take for this wilder, more primitive side to wane between them, but he wasn't complaining.

Amber suddenly stiffened, climaxing with a loud shout, and Desmon followed her over the edge. The pleasure just grabbed him, pulling him under, until he was thrusting into her, hard, fierce, following the pulse of his own release, but Amber was still there with him. Even out of his mind with ecstasy, he savored the way she shook in his arms. He loved that it was both of them drowning in this pool of pleasure, because without her there with him, Desmon knew it would've never felt this fucking good.

It took a long time for the ecstasy to fade while his dick still throbbed inside her, letting them come down together. The first thing Desmon felt after the storm was Amber's fingers, soft on his back, soothing the healing scratches. It was a gentle caress, a lover's caress, something far more human than wolf, and he loved that, too, maybe even more than the wolf sex moments before. He loved everything about her...and she was all his.

"I love you." He spoke it out loud against the curve of her neck, licking a healing bite, enjoying the tang of her blood still there. "We're going to survive this, Angel. It's going to work for us, we'll make sure of it."

"We will?" Amber asked, like she wasn't sure, either. It was still a lot to take in, and reality obviously grabbed her quickly in the come down. "What if I'm terrible at this? What about everything with the Goodwins? What if the pack hates me?"

"They just fought to save you. They'll love you. You're already an incredible werewolf, and we're going to be fine." Desmon believed it completely, more so than ever, because Miles had been right. The Nightwind pack was stronger now than they had been when he was a pup. "I promise."

"How can you promise that?" She pushed at his shoulder, trying to untangle herself from him, but Desmon wouldn't let her. "You don't know that, Des!"

"We'll have each other." He brushed Amber's hair off her forehead, and knew he was telling the truth. "It'll be enough. Nature says we're supposed to be together, and nature rarely lies."

"Okay." She reached up to caress his cheek, still rough with stubble. Her light gaze grew glassy with tears as she smiled and whispered, "I believe you."

The saga continues. Up next...Jazz

ALSO BY THE AUTHORS

Touching Ice (Cyborg Seduction Book 4)

Stealing Coal (Cyborg Seduction Book 5)

Redeeming Zorus (Cyborg Seduction Book 6)

Taunting Krell (Cyborg Seduction Book 7)

Haunting Blackie (Cyborg Seduction Book 8)

Loving Deviant (Cyborg Seduction Book 9)

Seducing Stag (Cyborg Seduction Book 10)

Falling for Sky (Cyborg Seduction Book 11)

VLG

Drantos (VLG Series Book 1)

Kraven (VLG Series Book 2)

Lorn (VLG Book 3)

Veso (VLG Series Book 4)

Lavos (VLG Series Book 5)

Wen (VLG Series Book 6)

Aveoth (VLG Series Book 7)

Creed (VLG Series Book 8)

Glacier (VLG Series Book 9)

Redson (VLG Series Book 10)

Trayis (VLG Series Book 11)

ZORN WORRIORS

Ral's Woman (Zorn Warriors Book 1)

Kidnapping Casey (Zorn Warriors Book 2)

Tempting Rever (Zorn Warriors Book 3)

Berrr's Vow (Zorn Warriors Book 4)

Coto's Captive (Zorn Warriors Book 5)

MATING HEAT

Mate Set (Mating Heat Book 1)

His Purrfect Mate (Mating Heat Book 2)

Mating Brand (Mating Heat Book 3)

RIDING THE RAINES

Propositioning Mr. Raine (Riding the Raines Book 1)

Raine on Me (Riding the Raines Book 2)

Claws And Fangs

MORE TITLES BY KELE MOON

BATTERED HEARTS Series M/F

Defying the Odds

Star Crossed

Crossing the Line

UNTAMED HEARTS Series M/F

The Viper

The Slayer

The Enforcer

EDEN Series

Beyond Eden M/M/F

Finding Eden M/M

Claiming Eden M/M

STANDALONE NOVELS

The Queens Consorts M/M/F

Starfish and Coffee M/M

Packing Heat M/M

SHORTS

A Kiss for Luck M/F

Mercy Bound M/F

ABOUT THE AUTHOR

LAURANN DOHNER

NY Times and USA Today Bestselling Author

I'm a full time wife, mother, and author. I've been lucky enough to have spent over two decades with the love of my life and look forward to many, many more years with Mr. Laurann. I'm addicted to iced coffee, the occasional candy bar (or two), and trying to get at least five hours of sleep at night.

I love to write all kinds of stories. I think the best part about writing is the fact that real life is always uncertain, always tossing things at us that we have no control over, but when writing you can make sure there's always a happy ending. I love that about being an author. My favorite part is when I sit down at my computer desk, put on my headphones to listen to loud music to block out everything around me, so I can create worlds in front of me.

http://www.lauranndohner.com

ABOUT THE AUTHOR

KELE MOON

A freckle faced, redhead born and raised in Hawaii, Kele Moon has always been a bit of a sore thumb and has come to enjoy the novelty of it. She thrives off pushing the envelope and finding ways to make the impossible work in her story telling. With a mad passion for romance, she adores the art of falling in love. The only rules she believes in is that, in love there are no rules and true love knows no bounds.

So obsessed is she with the beauty of romance and the novelty of creating it she's lost in her own wonder world most of the time. Thankfully she married her own dark, handsome, brooding hero who had infinite patience for her airy ways and attempts to keep her grounded. When she leaves her keys in the refrigerator or her cell phone in the oven he's usually there to save her from herself. The two of them now reside in Florida with their three beautiful children who make their lives both fun and challenging in equal parts–They wouldn't have it any other way.

http://www.kelemoon.com